Warwick's Mermaid

by

Ellie Gray

Warwick's Mermaid

Cover Art by *Diana Carlile*

The Wild Rose Press, Inc.
PO Box 708
Adams Basin, NY 14410-0708
Visit us at www.thewildrosepress.com

Publishing History
First Edition, 2021
Trade Paperback ISBN 978-1-5092-3773-9
Digital ISBN 978-1-5092-3774-6

Previously Published: Tirgearr Publishing, 2017
Published in the United States of America

Dedication

For David xxx

Prologue

Chloe MacGregor stared at the bright blue front door, not quite sure if she was willing it to open or remain shut. Cerulean Bliss. She had been drawn to the name, conjuring up images of a crystal-clear Mediterranean Sea, sandy beaches, and cloudless skies. Chris had appeared amused by her decision to choose the paint based on the name rather than the colour.

"Babe, if you want Cerulean Bliss for the front door, Cerulean Bliss is what we'll go for."

But when he'd returned from a boys' weekend away to find Chloe had painted the door, it had been a different story. He had flown into a rage, claiming she hadn't consulted with him on the colour and had gone behind his back, waiting until he was away to make changes to his house. That was the first time she had been on the receiving end of his anger; the first time she had been frightened and confused by his apparent about-turn on something he had previously agreed to. It hadn't been the last time.

She glanced at her watch, frowning when it showed only a minute had passed since she had last looked. The frown deepened when she lifted a hand to rub her eyebrow and saw how much her fingers were trembling. A gentle hand touched her forearm, and she looked up to meet her friend's calm gaze.

"Don't worry. It's going to be fine."

Chloe shook her head, unable to prevent her gaze from returning to the front door only twenty or so metres from where they were sitting in her car on this quiet, side street in the North Yorkshire seaside town of Scarborough. *What if he glanced around and saw her? What if he didn't?*

"What am I doing, Bekah?" She dropped her head in her hands, squeezing her eyes shut, and immediately wincing as that small movement resulted in more pain than it should have.

"The right thing, that's what." Rebekah Carter rubbed her friend's forearm. "Come on, Chloe. We talked about this."

"I know, I know we did." She lifted her chin, unable to prevent her gaze from returning to the door. "I just…I keep thinking about it, over and over. He's not always that bad, not really, and I think…I think maybe it was my fault."

She didn't have to see her friend's face to know she was angry; she could feel it radiating from her in waves. Rebekah remained silent, and simply reached across to pull down the sun visor in front of Chloe, lifting up the small flap covering the vanity mirror.

"There is nothing you could have done that would ever justify what he did to you. Nothing."

Chloe stared at her reflection, taking in the dark purple bruise circling her left eye—now bloodshot and half-closed—the ugly graze sweeping across her cheekbone, and further down to the swollen and split bottom lip. Without thinking, she drew the tip of her tongue over the injury, drawing in a sharp breath at the sting it produced.

She met her gaze in the mirror once more, silently acknowledging the confusion and uncertainty dulling their green hue. "I know. But it's not usually this bad. He pushes me around a bit sometimes, nothing major, and he says things…you know, usually when he's had a drink."

"That doesn't make it right. You know that." Rebekah blew out a long breath. "I can't believe you never told me."

Chloe avoided her friend's accusing gaze. What could she have told her? That Chris was proving her mother right? That she wasn't woman enough for any man?

"It doesn't matter now anyway. I—" She drew in a strangled breath as the front door opened and, shrinking down a little in her seat, she prayed he wouldn't glance down the street and recognise her car among all the others parked along the kerb.

Chris locked the front door before turning and sauntering down the garden path, tossing his keys in the air and catching them, his lips pursed in a whistle. She couldn't hear from this distance, but she knew he would be whistling the tune to whichever song had been on the radio before he left the house. She glanced at her watch once more; 8.15am on the dot. Chris was a creature of habit.

"Bastard." Rebekah thumped the dashboard, venting her anger as he got into his car without glancing left or right before driving off. "Look at him, acting as if he hasn't a care in the world. You should have let Sean come round last night and hammer ten bells out of him, see how *he* liked it."

Chloe gave a weak smile. "I don't suppose that

would have solved anything."

They sat in silence for a few minutes before Rebekah finally opened her door.

"So, come on then. Let's do it."

She bit her lip and immediately winced in pain, wishing she hadn't. Gingerly exploring her lip with her fingers, she saw they were stained with blood and, stifling a sigh, searched in her bag for a tissue.

"What if he comes back? What if he's forgotten something?"

"He's not coming back. He's gone to work." Rebekah nodded encouragement. "Come on, the sooner we get in, the sooner we get out. We'll only be a few minutes."

****

Two minutes later, Chloe was unlocking the door with trembling fingers, her heart thumping painfully in her chest as she pushed it open. Cerulean Bliss. It conjured up no happy thoughts for her now. It hadn't done from the moment Chris had returned from his weekend away. When she hesitated on the step, Rebekah gave her a gentle shove, propelling her into the hallway.

"Hey!"

"Well, we can't stand in the doorway all day." She glanced around. "Okay, so where first? In here?"

Her friend gestured to the living room, but Chloe shook her head immediately. She wasn't ready to face that room, not yet. Instead, she walked over to the bottom of the stairs and, after a moment's hesitation, shouldered her overnight bag and ran lightly up to the first floor. Ten minutes later she reappeared and joined Rebekah, where she was waiting patiently in the hall.

"Got everything?"

"Almost." She licked her lip, the sharp sting and coppery taste of blood reminding her why she was doing this. Taking a deep breath, she walked into the living room, her gaze immediately drawn to the coffee table. It looked as tidy as ever, with the magazines and books neatly stacked in one corner. In her mind's eye, she replayed the moment Chris had finally tipped over the edge.

It was football this time; football and beer. His team had lost and, downing his fifth can of beer, he had turned to her, obviously looking to pick a fight so he could vent his frustration. Chloe couldn't remember what it was he had said, but she had given a non-committal response before asking him if he wanted a coffee in a somewhat obvious effort to change the subject. But he hadn't let it drop, blocking her path as she tried to walk into the kitchen.

Her stomach rolled as she recalled Chris pushing his contorted face into hers, yelling at her through gritted teeth as he backed her up against the wall, knocking over the plant stand by the fireplace as he did so.

She closed her eyes. It was her fault. If she had just let him carry on, he would have calmed down eventually. But she hadn't. She had pushed him away, pushed at his chest as he crowded in on her. And that was all it had taken. Any ounce of self-control Chris might have had went flying through the window, just as she went flying when he grabbed her hair and threw her across the room.

She could remember lying on the floor in a daze, wondering what had happened, and Chris dragging her to her feet before punching her in the face. That was when she had fallen across the coffee table, her cheek grazing the corner as it tipped over and spilled the magazines to the floor. A kick to the ribs for good measure had followed, with Chris standing over her, his breath coming in harsh rasps, before he turned away and went upstairs, hissing, "You're not worth the effort."

"Chloe? You okay?"

Rebekah's gentle voice broke into her thoughts, and Chloe blinked, unable to speak for a moment. "Um…yes. I just need a couple of things from here."

She hurried over to a bookshelf and took a handful of books before casting a final glance around the room, sick with fear that Chris might return at any moment. There was very little here that she could call her own; Chris's minimalist taste left little room for any of her personal items. Anything she had bought herself had either mysteriously gone missing or been accidentally broken.

Sorry, babe, don't know what happened there. Never mind, it wasn't expensive, we'll get you something else.

"I think that's it. There's nothing else here I want." Following Rebekah out of the house, Chloe locked the door and posted the keys through the letterbox. With a final look along the street, she walked back to her car. She was worth more than that.

Chapter One

One Year Later

"Why did I let you talk me into this?" Chloe gazed reluctantly through the window as the taxi swept through the elegant wrought iron gates and along the gravelled drive towards the Grade 1 listed building. The pale stone walls appeared to glow as the setting sun cast its dying rays over the towering mansion, its many windows reflecting the burnished orange, as if the house were ablaze from within; an image that did nothing to lift her spirits.

"You know why." Lucie Craven opened the door as the taxi drew to a halt by the stone steps leading up to the impressive entrance. "I didn't want to come on my own, and you don't get out enough."

"Says who?" Chloe leaned into the front of the taxi to pay the fare. "Thanks very much. You can keep the change." Stepping out onto the gravel, she resisted the urge to ask the driver to turn around and take her home. Instead, she gazed after him as he drove away, before turning to follow Lucie into the hall.

Despite the high ceilings, the dark wood panelling gave the room an oppressive atmosphere, which wasn't helped by the endless rows of solemn-faced portraits scowling down at them as if in disapproval.

"Oh, for heaven's sake, Chloe. I didn't force you to

come, you know." Lucie gave an irritated sigh. "Stop being such a misery."

Chloe blinked in surprise. No, technically Lucie hadn't forced her to come, but she had subjected her to a constant barrage of texts and phone calls. Nevertheless, she had eventually agreed, and so she forced a smile to her lips "Okay, you're right, I'm sorry. Look, let's find out where we're supposed to be going."

A rather stout woman materialised, seemingly out of nowhere, the lace ruffle of her blouse accentuating a heavy bosom.

"Good evening, ladies." She cast a brief, practised eye over their proffered gold-embossed invitations. "If you follow the hallway down to the left, you will find the Rose Ballroom directly in front of you."

The two women obediently followed her instructions, their footsteps making little sound on the carpet.

"You look gorgeous in that dress, you know. It matches your eyes."

Lucie was once more all sweetness and light, and Chloe automatically glanced down, brushing her hands over the simple emerald-green velvet shift dress that skimmed her knees. She cast her friend a swift, knowing glance. Lucie was only ever happy when things were going her way, and it was something Chloe tended to forget. Why did she never learn?

"Come on, let's get this over with."

Despite her reluctance about the evening, she had to admit the ballroom looked amazing. Floor to ceiling windows ran the length of the room, allowing breath-taking views across gardens originally designed by

Capability Brown. The House was open to the public during the day, and Chloe had visited on several occasions over the years; knew the rooms boasted a fabulous collection of Chippendale, Sheraton, and French furnishings. This evening, however, all the antique furniture had been removed and replaced with modern, but nonetheless elegant, chairs and tables running along both sides of the room, and creating a natural dance floor in the middle.

A string quartet played discreetly on a small, raised dais in one corner, the musicians confidently holding their own against the conversation and laughter steadily filling the room. The room held the air of a bygone era, as if she had stepped through a portal into another, more genteel age. The timeless formal dress worn by the men, and the full-length ball gowns of the women swirling across the floor as they waltzed in the arms of their partners, simply added to the illusion.

Recognising no-one, Chloe bit her lip, once again wishing she hadn't allowed herself to be cajoled into attending the charity ball. Lucie knew she was a soft touch, especially when it came to charities for disadvantaged children, and that was the only reason she had allowed herself to be persuaded to attend a party where, with the exception of her friend, she would know no-one. She was only slightly reassured to find that, despite the flowing ball gowns whirling around the dance floor, there were a significant number of women who, like Chloe, had chosen not to wear full-on formal dress.

"Lucie, darling, you're late."

Chloe turned in surprise to see Lucie embracing a stocky, sandy-haired man whom she recognised instantly.

"Chloe, you look stunning." Lucie's husband leaned forward to kiss her cheek.

"Clive." She gave an uncertain smile. "I thought you couldn't make it."

Before he could respond, Lucie gave a tinkling laugh and an unrepentant wave of her hand. "Just a little white lie on my part." She tapped her husband's arm. "Don't be rude, darling. Aren't you going to introduce us? It's Luke, isn't it?"

She leaned forward to shake hands with the tall man standing politely by Clive's side.

"Lucie." Chloe stared at her friend. "You told me Clive couldn't make it. It's the only reason I agreed to come." She hated lies, white or otherwise, and Lucie knew that.

"Oh, for God's sake, stop making such a fuss." Things not going her way, Lucie began to twitch.

Chloe bit back an angry retort, reluctant to cause a scene. She turned to Clive when he briefly touched her elbow.

"Chloe, um…can I introduce Luke Warwick? He's recently moved to the area on business." Clive was clearly uncomfortable with his wife's duplicity but nodded encouragingly. "Luke, this is Chloe MacGregor."

Trying desperately to disguise her annoyance in front of this stranger, she forced a smile to her lips and automatically reached out to shake his hand. As his fingers closed around hers, she lifted her gaze to meet his and felt an unexpected thrill of awareness as their eyes met. He made no attempt to end the handshake, and seemed content to let her fingers remain lightly clasped in his until she pulled her hand free to tuck an imaginary strand of hair behind her ear, striving to mask her discomfort.

"Pleased to meet you, Miss MacGregor." His voice held a gravelly edge.

The immaculately cut dinner jacket accentuated his broad shoulders, hinting at a taut muscular body and, despite her three-inch heels, she had to tip her head back to meet his gaze. He smiled down at her, and again she experienced the unusual sensation of finding her heart beating a little faster than normal. Completely unnerved by such an unexpected and physical reaction to this stranger, she managed to nod politely and return his smile before turning to the others.

Following Lucie as she threaded her way through the row of tables, Chloe was acutely aware of Luke's presence close behind her. On reaching their table, she smiled her thanks when he pulled out her chair, waiting until she was settled before seating himself beside her. To her dismay, Lucie immediately struck up an animated conversation with a couple sitting at the next table, and Chloe glanced around, closing her eyes briefly, hoping she didn't look as desperately awkward as she felt. This was why it had been a mistake to allow herself to be persuaded to come tonight; she would stand out like a sore thumb—a singleton in a room full of couples or groups of single friends. Instead, she was tagging along playing gooseberry or, worse still, participating in what was beginning to look very much like a blind date.

She stifled a sigh. So, why *had* she allowed herself to be persuaded? Perhaps it was because she had smarted at Lucie's slightly barbed comment about behaving as if she were a sixty-year-old spinster instead of a twenty-eight-year-old woman, tucked up on the sofa with her dog and a mug of hot chocolate. More likely, it was a result of the conversation she had had with her mother earlier in the week; the one that had ended with Chloe shivering in horror when her mother told her they were two of a kind and that they needed to stick together. Her determination to prove her mother wrong simply looked like proving, once again, that Chloe's worst fears would be realised, and she was indeed her mother's daughter.

****

Luke relaxed back in his chair, his body angled towards Chloe, one arm resting casually on the table, the other along the back of his chair. In stark contrast, she was sitting bolt upright, her hands clasped tightly in her lap, and his gaze narrowed thoughtfully as he watched her battling with some emotion. He had been taken by surprise when he saw her walk into the room with Lucie, recognising her instantly as the girl he had been captivated by on the beach below his cliff-top cottage. He remembered how her auburn curls, tumbling down to the base of her spine, had shone brightly in the sunlight as she collected shells along the shore, oblivious to his gaze. And now here she was again; except tonight she was tense and uneasy, whereas on the beach she had seemed relaxed, carefree, and somehow ethereal.

"Red or white?"

She looked up in surprise and Luke smiled faintly, gesturing to the wine bottles sitting on the table. "Do you drink red or white?"

"Oh, er…white, please." She briefly met his gaze

before adding, "Can't stand red."

As he reached forward to pour her a glass, she snapped around to face him. "This isn't a blind date, is it?"

He favoured her with a curious glance, taking his time with pouring himself a glass of water before settling back into his seat. "I've just moved to the area. A friend suggested the ball and put me in touch with Clive, and I couldn't think of a good reason why not. He mentioned Lucie would be bringing a friend, but in answer to your question, no, I didn't understand it to be a blind date."

Chloe nodded and sipped at her wine, clearly unconvinced.

"I gather Lucie has persuaded you here under false pretences?" Aware that this was somehow a big deal for her, he frowned and leant forward. "Look, forget Lucie's intentions, blind date or otherwise. Even if I hadn't been invited as part of the group, you would still be sitting next to a stranger. Why don't we start again as two people who happen to meet up at a ball, safe in the knowledge that, after this evening, we don't have to see each other ever again if we don't want to?"

"Luke Warwick." He reached out his hand, holding her gaze.

After a brief hesitation, she took it, the tension visibly leaving her body as she smiled at him in relief. "Chloe MacGregor."

"That's better, Chloe MacGregor." He smiled back, relieved to see her begin to relax. "That's the first genuine smile I've seen from you all evening. It suits you."

His heart sank when she immediately dropped her

gaze with a frown, turning away from him to sip at her wine. *What had he said?*

He watched her curiously, surreptitiously, as she gazed around the room, seemingly avoiding his glance, and rolling her shoulders as if to ease tension. He was about to speak when she froze, her glass halfway to her mouth as she drew in a ragged breath. Luke glanced across to the far side of the room where her gaze was fixed, but could see nothing amiss. Turning back to her, he saw the frown creasing her forehead as she shook her head, obviously having some sort of internal conversation with herself. The next minute, her eyes widened, and he jumped in surprise when she shot to her feet, her chair falling backwards to the floor.

"Chloe?" Luke stood up beside her, his hand brushing her elbow to draw her attention from the far side of the room. "What is it?"

"Lucie, did you know Chris was going to be here?" She ignored him and turned to her friend, her voice oddly tight. The colour creeping along Lucie's neck and into her face was answer enough.

"Of course, I did. He suggested it actually." Lucie gave a shrug. "I don't see what the big deal is. You split up over a year ago. Get over it."

There was a long, tense moment and then, without a word, Chloe turned and walked away from them.

****

Weaving her way through the maze of tables, Chloe willed her shaking legs not to give way, and tried to keep one eye on Chris. *What had she been thinking?* She knew what Lucie was like—only interested in herself. She wouldn't put it past her to have invited Chloe simply to provide a bit of entertainment; to see what would happen when she saw Chris again and learned—by the look of his companion—that he was soon to be a father. Lucie had always been a bitchy troublemaker at school, but at other times she could be a good laugh, and had continued to make sporadic efforts to stay in touch with Chloe over the years. Efforts that Chloe had always accommodated, just as she had tonight. Well, not anymore. She had had enough. Lucie could go and take a running jump. With friends like her, who needed enemies?

Fingering her temple lightly as she recognised the beginnings of a headache, she absently took a sip from the glass of wine still clutched in her hand, while she lingered in the corner of the room with her back to the couple she was trying to avoid, waiting for them to move so she could make her escape. A quick glance over her shoulder left her struggling to draw breath as her eyes met those of her ex-boyfriend, a satisfied smile playing around his mouth as he began slowly and deliberately making his away across the room. She turned away, desperately trying to control the panic threatening to overwhelm her.

Why now? Why was he here now?

But she knew the answer to that. The court injunction she had served on him had expired just a couple of weeks earlier, and she had not applied for a renewal. She hadn't seen or heard from Chris for almost a year, and had been keen to draw a line under that part of her life, anxious to move on. Renewing the injunction would have meant acknowledging that he still had power over her.

"Chloe, it's good to see you; it's been a long time."

The once familiar voice made her nauseous, but

she turned around to face him, forcing a smile to her lips. She stiffened when he leaned forward to kiss her on each cheek. "This is Lisa, by the way." He gestured towards the girl at his side without taking his gaze from Chloe. "You look fantastic."

Ignoring his somewhat inappropriate comment, she turned to his girlfriend. "Lisa, it's nice to meet you. Gosh, it looks like congratulations are in order."

"I'm glad we've met up tonight." Chris carried on as if she hadn't spoken. "Always felt there was a little bit of unfinished business between us. You never did say goodbye, did you? Just dropped your keys through the door and served me with an injunction. Bit harsh, actually."

Chloe swallowed against the bile stinging the back of her throat. "Oh, I think you said goodbye enough for both of us, don't you?"

"Yes, well, no hard feelings, eh?" His eyes narrowed as if surprised at her defiant words.

"No, none at all." She gave a cool smile, acutely aware of his girlfriend and how awkward she must feel. That made two of them. "We clearly weren't right for each other. But it looks as if you two are doing well."

Lisa shot her a grateful smile and pulled at Chris's arm. "I think we should get to our table, don't you?"

Chris ignored her and simply shrugged off her arm until, with a faint blush stealing across her cheeks, Lisa turned and walked away.

"Weren't right for each other? After everything I put up with from you? Overlooking your *little problem* and standing by you, despite your uselessness?"

Chloe's carefully constructed confidence and feelings of self-worth wavered under his contemptuous gaze and the memory of all the hurtful things he had thrown at her time after time.

"I think maybe I'm not the one with the problem." It took some effort to keep her voice even, but she was determined to stand up to him.

His eyes widened slightly, and he took a slow step towards her, speaking so that only she could hear him. "Since when did you get to be so brave, Chloe? I think you'd better watch your mouth. No injunction to hide behind now."

It took everything she had not to shrink away from him as he stared her down, and after a few moments he gave a disbelieving laugh, glancing purposefully across at Lisa, now sitting alone at their table. "I think the proof that I wasn't the one with a problem is sitting right over there, don't you?"

And there it was. Proof indeed that she was the problem. Just like she'd always known. *Why had she even tried to deny it?* She could feel her legs begin to tremble, and fought to keep her face impassive, desperate not to let him know how much his words still hurt.

"There you are, darling. I thought I'd lost you."

Luke's hand at her waist gently pulled her into his side, and she automatically leaned against him, drawing comfort from his solidity, while at the same time wondering at his choice of words. She looked up at him in surprise, and he responded by dropping a soft, feather light kiss on her forehead. When he lifted his head, his gaze held hers for a moment, and she simply blinked up at him in something of a daze. This evening was taking an increasingly weird turn, and she was at a loss to explain what was happening. When Luke casually turned to the man observing this intimate scene in silence, Chloe realised she was grasping Luke's lapel and she uncurled her aching fingers, carefully smoothing the creased material in an effort to soothe her own confused thoughts.

"Luke Warwick." He held out his hand.

"Er…Chris. Chris Wilkinson." He winced slightly at the firmness of Luke's grip.

Luke nodded crisply, his gaze like ice. "Yes, I rather thought so. If you'll excuse us."

Without a backward glance, Luke took Chloe's elbow and she found herself being guided across the ballroom and back towards the entrance hall.

They walked in silence until, feeling her stomach roll with sudden nausea, she shrugged off his hand and ran down the corridor. Bursting through the cloakroom door, she was relieved to find it empty and bent over the hand basin, retching painfully for a few long moments. Shivering over the porcelain, she fought to control the sickness by drawing in long, deep breaths until the awful churning in her stomach gradually subsided. Feeling a little more under control, she turned on the cold-water tap, allowing the icy water to pour over her wrists as she rested her pounding forehead against the cool glass mirror.

A sob escaped her throat, catching her by surprise, and she pressed the back of her hand against her mouth, squeezing her eyes shut against hot tears. Damn him! Damn, damn, damn him! She risked a glance at her reflection, and saw the same, defeated expression she thought she had banished a year ago. She turned away quickly, her chin dropping onto her chest. *Don't allow him to do this. Only you can give him permission to make you feel worthless.*

Chloe straightened her shoulders. She had walked away from him and built a new life for herself. She would *not* let him ruin it now.

****

Luke waited in the corridor outside the cloakroom, feigning interest in the rather boring landscape hanging on the dark green wall. He wouldn't normally allow himself to get caught up in someone else's relationship problems, much less do so willingly. But he had watched the colour drain from Chloe's face as she recognised her ex, had seen her brazen it out when she had found herself confronted by him, and had been impressed by her spirit.

What surprised him had been the wave of anger he had felt at Lucie's complete lack of concern for her friend, and he had removed himself from the table, biting back a sharp retort in response to Lucie's comment about it all working out perfectly. He had intervened because he felt Chloe had been played a rotten hand tonight, and it did not sit well with his sense of fair play.

Still gazing unseeingly at the painting, he shook his head in wonder. *Why was he still waiting here?* He had intervened, had extricated her from a difficult situation and, by anybody's standards, had done his bit. *Why then did he feel this need to ensure she was all right? Why did he even think she needed his help?* He was acting out of character and he knew it. Luke Warwick never got involved; not emotionally anyway. Oh, he had fun, and enjoyed female company, but the emphasis was on fun and he was adept at finding women who equally had no interest in an emotional commitment.

Having made up his mind, he was about to leave when Chloe emerged from the cloakroom and turned to walk down the corridor without seeing him. Despite his better judgement, he strode after her and caught up with her as she walked out onto the front terrace.

Head down and smoothing her hands over her dress, Chloe's steps were slightly unsteady, and she started in surprise when he touched her arm lightly.

"Would you like me to take you home?"

Eyes glistening with sudden tears, she shook her head. "No, no. I'm fine, thank you. You don't need to stay with me."

That was his cue, his get-out-of-jail-free card. It was clear she neither wanted nor needed his help, and he could justifiably take his leave of her. But those emerald-green, tear-filled eyes unconsciously sent a different message, and he felt an overwhelming surge of protectiveness towards her.

"It's Friday night; you're going to have one hell of a wait for a taxi at this hour. My car is over there. I can drop you home, no problem."

Shaking her head, she pulled her phone from her bag and scrolled through various screens, obviously searching through her contacts. As she waited for the call to connect, a sharp breeze lifted her hair and she shivered, wrapping her free arm around herself. Without a word, Luke shrugged out of his dinner jacket and draped it across her shoulders, offering her a half smile when she looked up at him in surprise.

"No luck?" He asked a few seconds later, when she snapped her phone case shut.

"They can't send anyone for at least an hour." She closed her eyes in frustration, opening them again when he spoke.

"Then it's settled. Come on, I'll take you home." Without waiting for a response, he took her arm and led her towards his car, opening the door and gently pushing her in before walking around and getting in himself.

****

Your boyfriend is seeing other women. I thought you should know.

Chloe closed her eyes and leaned back against the cool leather seat, trying without success to push away the memories of the night she had confronted Chris.

Someone had sent the short, typed note to her work address. When she had shown it to Chris, he'd made no attempt to deny the accusation. Initially, he seemed to find it amusing, but Chloe's hurt and confusion, her need to know why, had incensed him.

"You really need to ask me why? Babe, you drove me to this, don't think you didn't," he spat the words in her face, his fingers gripping her shoulders painfully. "You want to know why? Fine, I'll spell it out for you. Because you're crap in bed. No, worse than that. You're…you're…I can't even put into words how bad you are. I'd get more pleasure from sleeping with a bloody mannequin than with you."

He'd looked at her incredulously, while she could only stare at him in speechless horror. "How can you not know, Chloe? I've told you often enough. I've only done what any man would do. You know, you really should get some help. Maybe a few lessons would teach you something. God knows, you need it."

Thrusting her away from him, he had stormed towards the door before turning back with one final

21

insult. "You have nothing to offer a man, Chloe. You're all pretty packaging, but open you up and you've nothing inside that a man needs or wants. You don't know how lucky you are to have me; anyone else would throw you out. You should be thanking me, not bloody snivelling on about me seeing other women. Especially when it's your fault."

Stifling a moan with the back of her hand, Chloe turned her face away, cheeks burning with humiliation at the memory.

"You okay?" Luke's soft voice broke into her thoughts.

She nodded, reluctant to enter into conversation, her gaze searching through the window for the familiar landmarks that would tell her she was nearly home.

It was another twenty minutes before they finally reached the tall hedge bordering her cottage, and Luke turned off the narrow lane onto the gravel driveway. It was easy to miss the turn-off to the cottage, but he showed no hesitation, bringing the car to a halt outside her front door.

The cottage stood in an isolated and secluded setting, several miles outside the gothic, North Yorkshire town of Whitby. With high hedges running along one edge of the garden, affording privacy from the road, and lower hedges bordering the three other sides, the cottage enjoyed breath-taking views over the cliff tops and out across the sea. Almost five miles from the local village, her nearest neighbour was a cottage similar to her own, a couple of miles further down the lane.

A sudden feeling of claustrophobia threatened to overwhelm her, and she fumbled for the door handle, scrambling out onto the gravel, and leaving Luke's jacket on the seat.

"Chloe, wait—"

"Thanks for driving me home."

She closed the car door, only just managing not to slam it in her haste, and turned to run across the lawn, away from the cottage. She quickly reached the bottom of the garden and let herself out through the gate and onto another path that led out towards the edge of the cliffs.

"Chloe!"

She paused and turned to see Luke standing by the car, his blond hair gleaming in the moonlight. *Why wouldn't he go?* Chloe hesitated, knowing she was being rude and ungrateful, but she was in no mood to make small talk with a stranger, even one who had gone out of his way to help her.

"I'm okay. I just need some air. You don't need to stay." She shouted over the breeze, impatiently brushing away the hair that whipped across her face.

"Wait!"

She shook her head and turned away, stepping onto the path that zigzagged its way down to the beach below. It was a clear night, and the moon shone brightly enough to light her way as she reached the bottom, pausing only to take off her sandals and drop them on a large rock, along with her clutch bag. Unencumbered, she walked along the shore, drawing in deep breaths of the sharp, salty air in a vain attempt to calm herself.

"Chloe."

She whirled around in surprise, her hand on her chest, stumbling slightly in the wet sand when she saw Luke walking towards her.

"For heaven's sake! What are you doing? Are you some kind of stalker or something? You don't need to follow me, I'm perfectly all right."

She turned and walked away, biting her lip when Luke appeared beside her, matching her pace but keeping a careful distance from her, seeming to have no problems walking in the deep sand.

"I'm not stalking you. I want to make sure you're okay. The tide's coming in fast; you shouldn't be down here, it's not safe."

"Don't you tell me when it is and isn't safe. I live here, I know this beach better than anyone." She couldn't believe the gall of the man, but a quick glance towards the ocean resulted in her heart thumping a little faster in her chest as she realised the tide was further in than she had anticipated. But she was damned if she was going to turn back on his say-so.

They carried on in silence for a few minutes until she couldn't contain herself any longer.

"Why did you do that?" Her lips were stiff with anger as she turned to face him.

"Do what?" His face seemed deliberately bland.

"You know what." She shook her head in irritation. "Kiss me like that in front of Chris, and pretend that we were…that we were…"

"Lovers?" He finished off for her. "I did it, firstly, because I thought Lucie had manoeuvred you into an intolerable position. And secondly, because I thought it probably best for you if your ex didn't realise you're still in love with him."

That stopped her in her tracks, her jaw dropping at his bald response.

"I am *not* in love with him," she managed,

eventually. "And I didn't need your help."

"Didn't you?"

"No, I didn't. You know nothing about me. I'm not some damsel in distress waiting for a knight in shining armour to rescue me." Her breath was coming in short, sharp gasps as she boldly faced the man standing in front of her. His penetrating gaze once again searched her face, a gaze that spoke of wanting to understand her. A gaze that had never once crossed Chris's face. Chris.

Chloe took a deep breath and turned her face away from Luke's scrutiny, unaware that she was speaking until she heard her words whispered into the cool, night air. "I'm worth more than that."

"Worth more than what?" His voice was gentle, and she closed her eyes against the tears that once again threatened to spill at his unexpected kindness. She reached down to pick up a shell, brushing the sand off, only to throw it away seconds later. She was acutely aware of Luke standing patiently beside her.

"You were wrong before, what you said. I'm not still in love with him. I'm not sure I ever was." She swallowed. "But he wanted me…I thought he wanted me. It was my one chance, you know? My one chance to prove her wrong…to show her I was…" Chloe broke off with a sigh.

"Worth more than that?"

She drew in a ragged gasp, staring at him in surprise.

He gave a half smile and shrugged. "You said you were worth more."

"But I wasn't, was I?" Tears streamed down her face as she covered her mouth with both hands to prevent the words from escaping, eyes wide at the admission she had made. Huge wracking sobs shook her shoulders as she stumbled along the beach. "I should have listened to my mother, but I was too stubborn, too desperate to prove her wrong. Turns out she was right after all. Oh, and how she revelled in that."

"Right about what? About Chris?"

Chloe shook her head, unwilling to admit such a shameful secret. She broke into a run, although whether it was to escape Luke or the past, she didn't know. He caught up with her in a few easy strides, catching her upper arm and turning her to face him gently when she refused to look at him. He said nothing, just stood holding her at arm's length, his thumbs caressing her skin in a soothing gesture.

"It's me. I'm not good…you know, in bed…with a man." She raised defiant eyes to meet his gaze, suddenly calm as she gave voice to her dirty little secret with a short, bitter laugh. "That's a bit of an understatement, actually. There's something not right with me. It was the same with my mother. I don't know, maybe it's hereditary or something. Anyway, she tried to warn me, but I wouldn't listen."

"Chloe—"

She shook her head quickly, wishing she were alone, that she had never started this conversation because now she couldn't stop. She had never spoken about this to anyone, not even Rebekah.

So why was she suddenly confessing her deepest, darkest secrets to a stranger? Maybe it was the thought of being able to unburden herself to someone who, to use his own words, she would never have to see again after tonight. Shaking off his touch, she turned towards the ocean, for once unmoved by the sight of the moonlight dancing across the restless waves.

"There's nothing physically wrong me, that's not the problem. But I hated him to touch me. I don't seem to have…what men need or want." Her voice dropped until it was barely a whisper. "Just pretty packaging, that's me. Chris said I was lucky to have him, no-one else would ever want me." She dipped her head, allowing the mass of coppery hair to fall forwards and hide her shame.

"Chloe, you can't believe that." Luke's fingers were gentle on her arm as he turned her to face him. "They're excuses for his own inadequacies; you know that, don't you?"

"No, you don't understand." She wrenched herself free from his grasp. "It's true, it was the same for Mum, and she tried to warn me. It was my own fault, I didn't listen. She was right; I'm worthless as a woman."

Luke reached out to cup her face with his hands, and he stooped a little to meet her gaze.

"You are *not* worthless. And that is not something a mother should ever, ever say to her daughter." He frowned and shook his head, his gaze holding hers. "I think it's more likely that your mother has the problem, not you."

He dropped his hands from her face, gently running them along her arms to lightly catch hold of her fingers. Her skin tingled from his touch, and she found herself unable to look away from the intensity of his gaze.

"You're not worthless," he repeated softly.

In a moment of madness, and without knowing what possessed her—only that she suddenly wanted him—Chloe reached up to bring his head down to hers, and kissed him. For a moment Luke didn't respond, but then his hands slipped around her waist to pull her into him, and he kissed her back. She was completed unprepared for the way her body reacted to his; deliciously alien sensations flooded through her, threatening to overwhelm her as she wrapped her arms around his neck, desperately wanting him closer.

Lost in his kisses, she blinked in confusion when he pulled away from her, carefully disentangling her arms from his neck as he took a step back.

"Chloe, I don't—"

She flinched and stumbled backwards, pushing his hands away when he reached out to her. *What was she thinking?*

"Wait—"

"No…no, you…" She gave a hiccup; a half laugh, half cry. "You just confirmed everything. I'm sorry. God, what an idiot."

"No, look, that's not what I meant."

"I don't care what you meant. I don't care what you say," she shouted, suddenly rushing forwards to push at his chest. "Leave me alone. I told you not to follow me, but you wouldn't listen. Why wouldn't you listen? Go away and leave me alone."

****

Luke made no attempt to stop her when she turned and ran back along the narrow stretch of sand, feet splashing in the water as the tide drew in. He passed a hand wearily over his face, wondering what on earth had just happened. The girl he had seen on the beach, the one who wandered along the shore collecting shells, and who danced and whirled and chased her dog, had seemed so carefree and happy. He'd been drawn to her, drawn to her ethereal beauty and other-worldliness. With her long, flowing skirts and wild curls, she couldn't have been further from the women he usually dated, but he'd been determined to catch her one morning and introduce himself. She'd been dressed more conservatively tonight, although he had been fascinated by the wide silver bands adorning her fingers, hinting at the girl from the beach beneath the conservative dress.

But this girl had issues. My God, did she have issues. *Who on earth told their daughter she was worthless?* He shook his head as a shudder of unexpected anger rippled through him. Chloe was beautiful and gentle, with a fragility that brought out his protectiveness. And yet he'd seen the inner core of steel, a quiet strength he admired. She was a strong young woman; a woman who had no idea of her own sexuality. When she'd kissed him, she had set his body aflame, and it had taken every ounce of self-control to push her away.

He sucked in a breath. It would have been easy to take advantage of her when she was so upset and angry, but he couldn't do it; it wouldn't have been right. Despite the feelings she aroused in him, he didn't want to be the reason she continued to doubt herself. And yet, in trying to do the right thing, he had hurt her.

While tonight had provided him with the perfect opportunity to meet her, it had also convinced him that he needed to stay well away from Chloe MacGregor. This was not a girl to mess around with; she'd obviously had more than enough of that to last a lifetime, and he was definitely not what she needed.

The tide was well in now, the waves rolling in quickly and soaking his feet. With a grim smile, he jogged across the beach to the path and slowly made his way up to the top of the cliff. When he reached the gate to her garden, he walked across the lawn towards the car, glancing at the cottage as he moved. It was in complete darkness.

Pulling open the car door, he sank onto the soft, leather seat.

Don't play with fire, Luke. Leave well alone.

Chapter Two

"Oh, Jasper, what was I doing? I made such a fool of myself last night."

The German Shepherd looked up expectantly on hearing her name, thumping her tail on the carpet as Chloe sank onto the sofa and dropped her head in her hands.

"I can't believe I kissed him. A complete stranger, and I kissed him!" She squeezed her eyes shut, her cheeks burning as she remembered vividly what it had felt like to be held in his arms, and her own completely unexpected response to his passionate kiss.

She looked up when Jasper whined and pushed a wet nose against her fingers.

"Okay, you're right; think positive." Chloe took a deep breath, and straightened up to address her dog. "So, lessons learned from last night. Number one, Lucie is a total bitch…excuse my language." She grimaced apologetically at Jasper. "But she is. She is definitely not a friend, and you'd better remind me of that the next time she rings or texts me."

"Lesson number two." She counted off on her fingers. "Chris…Chris is…"

Her chin wobbled and she paused, taking a moment to bite back sudden tears. Jasper shuffled closer as if sensing her distress, resting her head on Chloe's knees.

"Thank you, Jasper. I love you, too." She scratched Jasper's ears before nodding her head. "Lesson two. Chris is a complete and utter bastard, and obviously still has the power to hurt me, if I let him. But I won't, I can't. Otherwise, this last year has just been a complete waste."

"Lesson number three. Not everyone is like Chris; there are still some good guys out there. Guys like Luke Warwick, for instance." She paused, head on one side as she considered. "At least, I think he's a good guy. Not that I'll ever see him again, thank goodness."

She blew out a long breath. "Ohhhh, and lesson number four. Do not go around kissing said good guys. Just because I found out that I do actually like kissing some people, it does not change the fact that I am no good at the whole kissing and sex thing."

Chloe smiled and lifted Jasper's furry face, looking into the dog's beautiful, brown eyes. "And finally, lesson number five. The same lesson as every other day. I am a good person, and just because I'm rubbish in bed, it does not give someone the right to treat me like dirt."

"There." She let Jasper go and walked over to the window, looking out over the cliffs. "I think that's more than enough lessons for one day, don't you? How about going down to the beach?"

****

Jasper loped across the lawn and, barely pausing to give her mistress's hand a brief lick, galloped down the path towards the beach. Following at a more leisurely pace, Chloe couldn't suppress a smile at her dog's enthusiasm for life. Jasper still had the long-legged, floppy-eared look of a puppy. But already one ear had almost straightened and, at last, she was beginning to respond to Chloe's gentle discipline.

Shoving her hands deeper into her jeans pockets, she sighed, kicking barefoot at the sand. She had slept little last night, mortified that she had blurted out her shameful secret to a complete stranger and, even more confusing, unable to believe that she had launched herself on him. That kiss had awakened feelings she had never experienced before, but it was humiliating to realise that it had taken Luke only a few seconds to grow bored of her kisses, proving beyond doubt her lack of ability in that department. It shouldn't matter, but for some reason, it did. And no amount of telling herself otherwise would change that.

Resolutely pushing such negative thoughts away, Chloe wandered slowly along the shore, throwing sticks for Jasper. She stopped occasionally to pick up one of the hundreds of shells washed up every day on the beach, examining it carefully before either discarding it or placing it in the little cloth bag she had brought along for this purpose. She loved shells, and most days she managed to add one or two to her collection, hanging them on lengths of translucent fishing line at the windows to create the illusion they were floating, or placing them in clusters in the bathroom and on shelves and side tables. In the garden, she tied small shells to long lengths of string, hanging them on every available branch or fence pole to catch the perpetual breeze that blew in off the sea, and creating a permanent sound of the beach.

Deciding this particular shell was not quite right for her collection, Chloe dropped it back on the sand, shaking her head as the wind whipped her hair across her face. She stood for a while watching the clouds scurry across the morning sky, lost in thought and breathing in the crisp salty air. It wasn't working. The sea usually calmed her, but this morning she couldn't ignore the disquiet squirming in the pit of her stomach, something she hadn't felt for many months.

Lifting her hand to her mouth, she chewed on a fingernail. *Was it coincidence that, having not seen him for almost a year, Chris had turned up just two weeks after the injunction had expired?* She blinked back tears. No. He'd even mentioned it last night. *Had it been a threat?*

"Looks like we could be in for a storm."

Chloe started in alarm and turned quickly, expecting to see Chris. She gasped in surprise and relief when she saw Luke walking towards her, rugged and handsome in faded blue jeans and a navy fisherman's sweater. His chin was dark with stubble and his blond hair ruffled by the wind. She looked away, acutely aware of the sudden frantic racing of her heart.

"This is a private beach." Her voice was cold, and her lips tightened when her disloyal dog bounded around Luke, jumping up at him playfully. "Jasper, come here."

"Hello, boy. Have you brought a stick for me?" He bent and made a fuss of the dog, looking up at Chloe with a grin. "At least someone's pleased to see me."

"She's a girl, not a boy," she said, reluctant to enter into conversation, but out of respect for her beloved dog, unable to allow him to continue under the misconception that Jasper was male.

"Oh, is she?" He gave her a quizzical grin. "I just

assumed…you know…Jasper's a boy's name."

When she continued to glower at him in silence, he took the stick from the dog and threw it for her to chase before turning back to look at Chloe, his head angled slightly to one side.

"Are you okay?" Although he smiled, his pale green eyes were watchful and wary.

"This is a private beach." She repeated, her voice sounding wooden even to her own ears. "And like I said last night, I don't appreciate being stalked."

He continued to stare at her in silence before turning and gesturing to her cottage, the roof of which was just visible high up on the cliffs.

"You live in Smuggler's Keep, which allows you access to this beach, I presume?" When she nodded, he pointed to the cottage on the cliffs at the opposite end of the beach. "Am I right in thinking, then, that whoever lives there is also allowed to use the beach?"

She frowned. "Fulmar Cottage? Yes, that's right, but no-one has lived there for months."

"Eleven months, to be exact," agreed Luke, a slight smile tugging his lips when her eyes widened in surprise. "I believe that's what the estate agent told me when I bought the place three weeks ago."

Chloe's jaw dropped and she took an unconscious step backwards. "What? But you can't. No-one lives there, it's empty."

Her cottage and this beach were her own private sanctuary; a place of blissful solitude that gave her somewhere to escape to. She didn't want to share that with anyone, especially not Luke Warwick.

His eyes narrowed as he observed her somewhat panicked reaction, and he held out a hand.

"Is it really so bad having me as a neighbour?" Getting no response whatsoever from her, he dropped his hand and continued in a soft voice. "Look, we seem to have started off on the wrong foot, which is probably my fault. Why don't we start again? Come up to the cottage for a coffee?"

Chloe simply stared at him, unable to take her eyes from his face, unnerved and confused by the maelstrom of feelings whirling around her head. Part of her desperately wanted to say yes, to spend some time with this man who made her feel things she'd never felt before; made her feel like a woman. But another, far more sensible, part of her warned that this time would be no different.

That part of her also sensed there was a real danger of her falling for him. *How could she not?* Just look at him—all rugged good looks, urbane manner, and the body of a Greek god. She would fall for him and he would do one of two things: backtrack, horrified that she had misunderstood his gesture of friendship; or start a relationship with her and find out, like Chris, that she was a failure as a woman, in the most important sense.

She felt a sharp tug on her sweater and looked down to find Jasper pulling at her, asking for the stick to be thrown.

"I…I've got to go. Come on, Jasper, it's time to go home."

For the second time in twenty-four hours, she left Luke alone on the beach. Only when she reached the top did she allow herself to look back. He was standing where she had left him, picking absently at the loose bark on Jasper's stick. As she watched, he threw it into the sea, his frustration obvious, before turning to glance up at her as if suddenly aware of her scrutiny. Chloe quickly backed away, out of sight, her heart pounding.

Where was her safe place now?

****

The storm Luke had predicted finally broke directly overhead in the early evening, bringing gale force winds and driving rain. Although it was only six o'clock, Chloe turned on the lights and stood at the window, gazing out in fascination at the turbulent sea, its charcoal grey waves reflecting the ominously dark sky as they crashed against the cliffs below. The wind howled around the cottage, shaking the windows as if trying to force its way in, and she turned to frown at Jasper as the dog whined and scratched at the front door, asking to be let out.

"Really? You waited until the storm hit before deciding you need to go out?" She shook her head at the dog, rolling her eyes when the only response was a further whine and more scrabbling at the door.

Biting her bottom lip in irritation, she glanced once more through the window; there was no way the storm was going to blow over any time soon. She unlocked the front door with an impatient sigh and turned to the dog.

"You're on your own, kiddo. Make it quick."

Jasper hesitated on the step, looking back at Chloe as the rain blew in on the wind, before deciding to make a run for it. She made straight for the cover of the bushes at the bottom of the garden, and Chloe pushed the door almost closed, peering around the edge as she waited. After a few minutes, she pulled the door open wider to shout for her dog, gasping at the sudden blinding flash of lightning and simultaneous crack of thunder. Chloe nearly leapt out of her skin in fright, and at the same time saw Jasper flee through the gate with a yelp of pure terror.

"Jasper! No!"

Without thinking, she grabbed the flashlight hanging on a hook by the door, and raced after her, the beam catching Jasper as she fled down the cliff path. Chasing after the dog, Chloe's heart skipped several beats as she slipped and slithered down the treacherously muddy path, but somehow made it in record time to the beach. The rain lashed at her in the ever-darkening sky, making it difficult to see, and she held a hand in front of her face to shield her eyes as she repeatedly shouted for Jasper.

Stumbling over the rocks clustered around the bottom of the cliff where it jutted out into the roaring, boiling sea, she swung her torch back and forth, desperately hoping for a glimpse of her dog. The wind blew an arsenal of gritty, wet sand into her face, and she turned away from the stinging bullets only to freeze in terror when she saw a towering wall of water rolling towards her. She screamed and instinctively dropped to her knees, arms folding over her head as she waited for the wave to hit. To her relief, it crested several feet in front her, crashing to shore and rushing forwards to sweep her off her knees. She floundered in the water for a few seconds before her wildly kicking legs found purchase, and she managed to drag herself up the beach, fighting against the pull of the water as it tried to sweep her back with it.

Hacking coughs wracked her body as she gulped in deep breaths of air and tried to get her bearings, casting nervous glances towards the angry ocean as she moved higher up the beach. It was almost completely dark now and she squinted into the driving rain, suddenly remembering the flashlight hanging from the strap around her wrist.

She had been searching for what seemed like hours, although in reality could have only been a few minutes, and Chloe was exhausted and frozen, her voice hoarse from shouting over the storm. Stumbling once again, she fell onto one knee and sank down onto the sodden sand, trying desperately to catch her breath as she choked back a sob. It turned into a frightened cry when she felt a hand dragging to her feet. She spun around to find herself gazing into pale green eyes blazing with anger.

"What the hell are you doing?" Luke yelled over the howling wind.

"Jasper…I can't find Jasper."

"The dog?" He stared at her as if he couldn't believe he'd heard her correctly. "You're out here looking for your dog?"

"Please, Luke. You've got to help me find her." She turned away to sweep the flashlight across the inky darkness.

"Are you crazy?" He caught her arm, turning her around to face him again. "No way. We need to get out of here."

"Fine! You go then." She pulled her arm from his grasp.

The wind tore the words from his mouth before they could reach her, but she was left in no doubt what he thought about her determination to stay on the beach. Cursing fluently, he ripped off his full-length waterproof coat, grappling with it in the wind as he forced her arms into the sleeves.

Shooting a final, fierce gaze towards her, Luke turned away and they began searching for Jasper, swinging their flashlights back and forth, and shouting for the terrified animal. Several times the tremendous force of the wind knocked Chloe completely off her feet and, inadvertently straying away from Luke, she lost her footing on a rocky outstretch as another viciously strong gust threw her against a large rock. Almost blacking out as pain lanced through her shoulder, the stinging rain ensured it was only a momentary loss of awareness. Grimacing in agony, she forced herself upright as Luke appeared at her side, putting his mouth close to her ear so she would hear him.

"Come on. I think I've found her."

He pulled her forwards, sweeping the torch beam from side to side until he saw again the brief flash of orange reflected in Jasper's eyes when the light played across her. Weak-kneed with relief, Chloe ran forward and found the dog whimpering in terror, huddled against a small group of rocks at the base of the cliffs. Somehow, Luke managed to lift the dog, hefting her over his shoulder, and throwing his other arm around Chloe's waist when her knees threatened to buckle. A quick glance towards the path to her cottage confirmed it was cut off by the tide and, as the huge waves crashed around them, he urged her to hurry; they needed to make it to the far side of the beach before that, too, was cut off.

The sea swirled around their thighs as they waded towards the path, waves crashing over their heads and knocking them to their knees several times, but at last they clambered onto the path and up to the top of the cliff.

****

Luke gently pushed Chloe into the cottage before leaning back to close the door on the storm and allowing Jasper to slide from his shoulder to the floor. Trying to catch his breath, he closed his eyes, grimacing at the throbbing ache in his legs, and wanting nothing more than to sink to the floor himself. Instead, he forced himself upright, turning his head away with a grimace as Jasper shook herself, sending sand and water flying across the kitchen.

Thanks, Jasper. That's really great."

Chloe appeared beyond speech, and was shivering uncontrollably. He guided her through to the living room to stand by the fire while he threw on more logs, before turning to her and gently peeling off the large, dripping coat.

"Hey, it's okay, we're safe. We made it." He smiled as she looked up at him, exhaustion clearly written across her face, and he brushed the strands of wet hair from her cheeks. His smile turned into a frown when he looked down at her bare feet. "Where are your shoes? Did you take them off already?"

"I think I lost my slippers in the sea."

"Your slippers? What…are you joking?" He stared at her. "You weren't out looking for Jasper in your slippers?"

Chloe shrugged as if it were the least of her worries. "I wasn't planning for Jasper to run off. She bolted and…and I went after her."

He opened his mouth to respond and then gave up, unable to think of a single thing to say to that. "Right.

Well, you need to get out of those wet clothes for a start. Wait here."

He returned to find her kneeling by the fire, hugging Jasper to her, her face buried in the dog's wet fur. Jasper herself appeared none the worse for her adventure.

"Here, there's a towel for your hair." He handed her a towel as she struggled to her feet, and passed a hand over his face as rivulets of sea water and rain dripped down from his own soaked hair.

"Are you wearing anything underneath that?" He plucked at her sweater, frowning when she bent forwards to dry her hair and winced in obvious pain. "You okay?"

"Yes. And yes." She dropped the towel on the sofa and began trying to pull her jumper over her head, but stopped with a muffled cry.

"What is it? Are you hurt?"

"I think I banged my shoulder at some point." She bit her lip, gesturing to her left arm, and began trying to wriggle out of her sweater using just one arm.

Luke hesitated, trying to gauge her reaction to his next question. "Do you want me to help?"

She paused in her efforts with a sigh, unable to meet his gaze.

"I think you're going to have to." Slight colour tinged her pale cheeks as she nodded and stepped closer to him, lifting one edge of the sweater, and waiting for him to lift the other. He gently pulled the sweater up over her head, wincing when she hissed in pain as he eased her arm from the sleeve.

"Here, let me take a look."

He was unable to bite back an explicit curse when

she turned her back to him. Beneath the thin straps of her vest top and bra, blood was oozing from a large cut across her shoulder blade, and already the whole area was bruising.

"How the hell did you manage that?"

He didn't wait for an answer. It had got to the point where he was working on automatic pilot, and he simply retrieved his first aid kit from the bathroom. In silence, he deftly cleaned and dried the ugly wound, applying butterfly strips and a sterile dressing before helping her into his warm, dry bathrobe.

He gave her a quick, searching glance before walking through to the kitchen. When he returned, he saw she had removed the sodden jeans and was once more snuggling next to Jasper. She looked up when he spoke her name softly.

Luke handed her a couple of painkillers and a glass of water, before taking the empty glass from her and replacing it with another glass, half-filled with a rich, coppery liquid. "Here. It's probably not what the doctor would advise, but I think it's acceptable in the circumstances."

"What is it?"

"Brandy." He cut off what was clearly going to be a refusal. "Drink it."

Draining his own glass, he closed his eyes and rested his forehead on the mantelpiece, fighting against the exhaustion making his arms and legs feel like lead weights.

He opened his eyes to see her obediently draining the glass, finishing the last drop with a grimace of distaste; the gesture brought the ghost of a smile to his lips. A sudden shiver took him by surprise, and he glanced down, suddenly realising he had not yet changed into dry clothes.

Come on, Luke; keep moving.

He pushed himself away from the fire and went through to the kitchen, returning with a steaming mug of coffee for Chloe, before forcing himself up the stairs to his bedroom.

His bed had never looked more inviting, and he fought against the urge to collapse onto it and bury his head in the soft pillows. That would have to wait. Not even daring to sit down for a moment, he quickly changed into a clean, dry shirt and jeans. A quick splash of water over his face in the bathroom left him feeling slightly less fatigued, and he leaned briefly on the basin, staring at his reflection in the mirror.

So much for staying away from Chloe MacGregor.

He had been unable to resist going down to the beach this morning when he saw her, despite his better judgement. And now this! Within twenty-four hours, she had managed to turn his life upside down. He closed his eyes, his heart thudding in his chest as he recalled seeing the flickering torchlight down on the cliff path. She could have been killed; they both could. *Did she have a death wish or something?*

Chloe hadn't moved when he returned and, despite almost sitting on top of the fire, he could see her teeth chattering slightly in her deathly pale face.

"Are you still cold?"

She looked up at him and nodded. "I can't get warm."

"I'll run you a bath. It might help warm you up."

****

Stepping carefully into the steaming water, Chloe

44

sank back to rest her head against the tiles, stifling a cry of pain as her injured shoulder pressed against the porcelain. Folding one of the soft fluffy towels to cushion her shoulder, she gingerly leaned back once more, this time with a sigh of relief. The storm continued to rage outside, the rain hitting the bathroom window so hard she wondered if it might crack the glass. The eaves in the attic groaned as the timber shifted in response to the force of the wind battering the cottage.

Closing her eyes wearily, she had a sudden memory of the towering wall of water rolling towards her, and she snapped her eyes open, sitting up quickly enough to cause a mini tidal wave of her own in the bath.

Unsettled, in pain, and unable to relax, she was gingerly drying herself ten minutes later when she heard a knock on the bathroom door.

"I've put a shirt of mine outside the door for you to wear. It's all I've got, I'm afraid." Luke's voice floated through the door. "I'll be downstairs if you need me."

Chloe limped down the stairs a few minutes later, the bathrobe tied tightly over the large, brushed cotton shirt that reached to mid-thigh. Walking into the living room, she saw him crouching next to Jasper, scratching the dog's ear, and talking to her softly.

"Is she okay?"

"She'll be fine." He looked up, eyeing her critically. "How are you doing? Any warmer?"

"Yes, thank you." She avoided his gaze. While the hot bath had warmed her outwardly, she still felt chilled to the bone, and every inch of her ached as she sank into the armchair closest to the fire.

Glancing across at Luke, she felt a stab of guilt; he looked exhausted. Once again, he had stepped in to help her, although perhaps *help* was something of an understatement this time.

"I'm sorry. I don't know what to say. Thank you probably doesn't cover it."

When he didn't respond, she looked up and was surprised to see him clearly struggling to keep his anger in check. When he finally spoke, his voice was low, and the words clipped.

"I can't believe you would be that bloody stupid." His fierce gaze dried any words of protest she was about to utter. "Do you realise how dangerous that situation was?"

When she remained silent, he turned away and threw another log on the fire, causing sparks to snap and fly up the chimney.

"You do not risk your own life like that for a dog."

"But you did."

He turned from the fire to look at her, one hand on the mantelpiece.

"It wasn't Jasper I was risking my life for."

His soft voice sent a tingle along her spine, and she met his gaze, her heart thumping in her chest. She shook her head with a half-smile, knowing he wouldn't understand.

"I couldn't just leave her, and I'd do it again. Every time."

"I know you would." He turned away and took a deep, steadying breath before looking back at her with the intense gaze that was becoming familiar. "And that's what bloody frightens me. If I hadn't seen your flashlight when I did, you wouldn't have gotten off that beach alive."

Chloe had been on the receiving end of Chris's anger so many times, but this was different. Luke's anger was born out of fear; fear for her safety. It had been stupid of her to go down to the beach in such a storm and at high tide, but she had been acting on instinct. Even if she had had time to think, she knew she would still have gone after Jasper. But Luke? Luke had risked his life for her today, and had shown such care and concern for her since they got back to his cottage, putting her needs before his own. For the first time in her life, she felt cared for.

"I'm sorry," she whispered, suddenly overwhelmed by conflicting emotions. She blinked away the tears suddenly blurring her vision. "I know you're right."

His expression softened and he nodded, walking over to pull her from the chair. "Come on, you're exhausted. The spare room is made up ready."

****

Luke slowly made his way downstairs, desperately wanting to sleep but knowing he would only lie there tossing and turning, his mind in overdrive. He moved over to the window and pulled back the curtain to peer outside, but could see only his own reflection, pale and ghostly, his face distorted by the rivulets of rain being driven across the glass. He let the curtain drop and turned away to pour himself more brandy. He downed the measure in one long swallow, hissing as the liquid burned into his stomach, then poured himself another and settled into the chair Chloe had recently vacated.

Easing himself back against the cushions, he stretched out his long legs towards the fire. His gaze fell upon Jasper, curled up peacefully as she slept in front of the fire, and he felt a sharp stab of fear in the pit of his stomach at the thought of how close Chloe had been to becoming trapped on that beach.

He shook his head and took another long swallow; it was only blind luck that he had seen her flashlight at all.

What if he hadn't decided to catch up on that paperwork? What if the paperwork had been here on his desk instead of in the boot of his car? What if, on pulling open the kitchen door, he had thought better of going outside?

It had been the height of the storm and he had contemplated leaving it until the morning, but in the end, had shrugged on his coat and boots and sprinted across the drive to his car, muttering to himself that the cottage was seriously lacking a garage.

A small cluster of trees blocked Chloe's cottage from view, and the cliffs were too high to allow Luke sight of the beach from here. It was sheer coincidence that, as he ran across the drive, Chloe had been scrambling down the only part of the cliff path visible to him. A flash of light in his peripheral vision made him pause as he reached for the car door, and he turned his head, blinking away the driving rain and gasping as the wind tore his breath away. Deciding it must have been more lightning, he had been about to turn back to the car when he saw again the wavering flicker of light, and he stood rooted to the ground while his brain struggled to process what his eyes were telling him. Somebody was out on the cliff path with a flashlight, and that someone could only be Chloe. That realisation sent him sprinting back to his cottage to grab his own flashlight, before racing down to the beach without a second thought.

But what if he'd gone out to get his papers a few minutes earlier or later? He wouldn't have seen that tell-tale flash of light. What if…?

He swallowed another mouthful of brandy. It was turning into one hell of a weekend, and he still hadn't done his paperwork. Suddenly overcome with weariness, he drained his glass and made the fire and the cottage safe, before climbing the stairs to his room. Just before turning in, he padded across the landing and quietly opened the door to the spare room to check on Chloe. He blinked in surprise when he saw her wrapped in a blanket and sitting in front of the small fireplace with her knees drawn up to her chin, shivering violently. He moved quickly to her side, frowning in concern.

"Chloe, what is it? What's the matter?"

"I'm…so…cold." Her teeth were chattering so hard it was difficult to make out her words. "I can't seem to…get warm."

The fire was still burning and giving off a substantial amount of heat in the small bedroom. Luke glanced at the bed and then at Chloe, considering his options. After a moment, he dragged the old over-stuffed armchair from the corner of the room, placed it at the fireside and pulled the duvet off the bed.

"Come here." He sat down in the chair and beckoned to her.

She looked up from her position on the floor, clearly confused.

"Come here," he repeated. 'sit on here with me; I'll put the duvet around you."

"What? No." She blushed despite the shivers

wracking her body, eyeing his t-shirt and jogging bottoms.

"Just…" He closed his eyes briefly, biting back his frustration. "Body heat is the best way to get you warm. I don't know what else to try if the fire isn't warming you up. I'm guessing the bed isn't an option."

"Come on, I'm not going to bite."

After a brief hesitation, Chloe pulled the blanket tighter around her before edging onto his knee, pulling her own knees once more up to her chin, cheeks flaming.

"Well, at least it's brought some colour to your cheeks." Luke tried to lighten the mood and ease her discomfort, briskly wrapping the duvet around them both. "Mind your shoulder."

He was shocked by how cold her body felt against his, and he eased the blanket loose from her grip and began gently chafing her arms, trying to warm her up. After a while, he could feel her begin to relax against him as the heat from his body gradually seeped into her frozen limbs, her head growing heavy on his shoulder. Half asleep, she shifted on his knee, pressing closer and slipping her arm around his waist. Luke closed his eyes, fighting against the sensuality of the moment and his desire to kiss her.

Chloe looked up at him in the flickering firelight, her eyelids heavy with sleep. "I'm sorry for being such a nuisance. I know you're angry with me."

Luke sighed and shook his head slightly. "Promise me you won't ever do anything like that again. Next time, you ring me, all right? Anything like that happens again and you ring me." He cupped her face with his hand, forcing her to meet his gaze. "Promise me." His voice was insistent.

Her eyes widened in surprise. "I promise."

After a moment, unable to stop himself, he bent his head and dropped a soft, brief kiss on her lips. "Are you warmer now?"

When she nodded, he gave a reluctant smile. "Then we'd better get some sleep."

He carried her over to the bed, wanting more than anything to lay down beside her and pull her into his arms. But instead, he straightened the duvet over her and returned to his own cold and empty bed.

How on earth had this woman so quickly become so important to him? It wasn't part of the plan.

****

Chloe stretched her arms above her head, lazily wondering why her room was so bright behind her eyelids this morning. *Had she forgotten to close her curtains?* The movement brought a stab of pain to her shoulder blade, and she opened her eyes with a snap. Momentarily disoriented, she sat up and stared around the room, wondering where on earth she was. A second later, the events of last night came flooding back, and she eased back on the bed, her eyes drawn to the chair sitting next to the fireplace, her cheeks flaring with colour as she remembered snuggling against Luke. He'd kissed her; a gentle, sensual kiss, so different from the forceful, demanding kisses she'd experienced with Chris. And the feeling of his hands stroking her arms, coaxing warmth into her body…

She rolled over to sit on the edge of the bed, stalling those thoughts quickly. Better not read too much into what had happened last night. Gazing around in an effort to think of something—anything—else, she smiled with pleasure. It was a beautiful room. Original seascapes adorned the fresh, white walls, and the sparing use of blue and natural wood furnishings served to create a calm, clean room. She ran a thoughtful hand across the crisp white bed linen before noticing her own freshly laundered clothes lying over the huge ship's chest standing beneath the window.

Time to get dressed.

****

The door to Fulmar Cottage stood wide open, and the breeze blowing through the house was sharp and fresh, bringing with it the haunting cry of seagulls that Chloe loved. Luke was whistling softly as he busied himself in the kitchen, but he looked up as Jasper gave a short bark of delight when she walked stiffly through the doorway.

"Hey, good morning."

"Morning." Chloe smiled, suddenly tongue-tied in his presence, and grateful for the distraction as she bent to fuss over her dog. When she looked up, she found he was watching her and she straightened, hovering uncertainly near the door.

He took a step forward before seeming to change his mind and, instead, leaned back against the work surface, folding his arms.

"How are you feeling this morning?"

"I'm okay," she shrugged. "A bit shaky; my shoulder's a bit sore, but I'm okay."

He nodded, and pulled out a chair for her at the scrubbed, pine kitchen table. "Come on, have some breakfast."

She watched as he moved around the kitchen; for such a powerful man, he moved with surprising grace and economy of movement. He brought over a fresh mug of coffee, a plate of croissants, and a couple of painkillers, before pulling up a chair to sit opposite her.

"Here, these should help."

"Thank you." She swallowed the pills gratefully. "What about you? How are you after yesterday?"

"Oh, I'm fine," he dismissed with a shrug and a smile. "A little tired perhaps. An aching back, because your dog is no lightweight, but I'm fine."

They sat in companionable silence, drinking coffee, eating croissants, and listening to the soothing sounds of the gulls and the waves crashing on the shore far below. Luke seemed lost in thought, and Chloe eyed him surreptitiously; his eyes were such an unusual shade of green, so different from her own bright green cats' eyes. Despite his fair, naturally blond hair, he had a deep, golden tan and looked to be in great physical shape.

"You still think I'm an idiot, don't you?"

He favoured her with an amused glance. "I wouldn't say you were an idiot."

"But you think it was stupid to go after her like that." She pressed him for an answer.

"Going out to look for your dog in a rain shower is one thing; going down to that beach in the middle of a raging storm is quite another." He just about managed to keep the impatience out of his voice.

"But—"

"Let's agree to disagree, shall we?" He cut her off with a smile, bringing the conversation to an end as he rose from the table to refill her mug.

"Okay." She stared through the window at the pale blue cloudless sky. "It's such a gorgeous morning. It's difficult to believe it was so awful last night."

"It was after a storm like last night that this part of the cliff got its name, so I'm told."

"McBride's Point?" She began to laugh. "Ah, so you've heard about the wonderfully romantic, but somewhat unlikely story we have around here for the tourists."

"You don't believe it?"

"What? And you do? Oh, come on, Luke." Her grin widened when he returned her disbelieving stare with a bland expression. "Okay, okay. Let's make sure we're talking about the same story here." She shifted in her seat as if settling herself for the story.

"So, two hundred or so years ago, Captain McBride—a sea captain, obviously—and his young wife lived here in Fulmar Cottage, probably called something else back then."

Luke's lips twitched as she waved her heavily ringed hands expressively.

"Now, whenever Captain McBride was due back from a voyage, his wife would watch for his ship, waiting for him to come home. Anyway, one particular day there was a terrible storm, much like yesterday as you said, and Mrs. McBride was waiting for her husband's ship. It got caught in the storm a few miles from port and she could do nothing but watch it go down. Of course, there were no survivors and so, unable to live without him, she threw herself from the cliffs and was found on the rocks below. It's been called McBride's Point ever since...There, how did I do?"

"Very good," he laughed, and shook his head. "You summed it up very succinctly. A tragic tale, indeed."

"But you can't believe it's true?" Her eyes narrowed as she tried to gauge his expression. "It was probably a terrible accident and she fell over the edge of the cliff. I imagine it's easy enough to do."

"You're a funny girl, Chloe MacGregor," said Luke softly.

"I just don't believe in the whole 'true love, can't live without you" thing." She shrugged uncomfortably, catching her breath at the seriousness of his gaze, and finding herself unable to look away. She was only too aware of her heart beating hard against her ribcage.

"Just because you haven't experienced it, doesn't mean that it can't exist, does it?" He gave a crooked smile.

"I can't believe you think the whole McBride thing is true." She chose not to answer his question directly.

"I wouldn't dismiss it entirely out of hand. I don't see any reason why it wouldn't be true," said Luke quietly. "I think anyone who has truly been in love would understand the depth of despair Mrs McBride might have felt."

Chloe remained unconvinced and dropped her gaze with a slight shake of her head, absently tracing the delicate whorls of a knot in the wooden table. With a disconcerting stab of jealousy, she wondered whom Luke had loved so much to cause him to sympathise with the young woman from the tragic story.

"Have you ever felt like that about someone?" She kept her eyes cast downwards, inwardly wincing at her audacity in asking such a personal question.

"No," he said, after a moment's hesitation. As she lifted her head, he interrupted whatever she was about to say. "But I have seen the incredible love my grandparents shared."

She heard the sincerity in his voice and frowned, thinking of the love she knew existed between Rebekah and Sean. Maybe love like that really did exist; just not for her. She knew without a shadow of a doubt that she was made differently. She didn't have it in her to draw that depth of feeling from someone else.

Luke reached out across the table, not for her hand, but to lay his palm flat on the smooth wooden surface.

"But I also saw the dreadful pain and heartache that happens when two people want different things, as my mother and father did when their marriage failed. I don't ever want to cause someone to hurt that badly, and that's the reason why I've not met anyone I want to fall in love with. I've worked damned hard to build up a successful business and I'm not ready for a long-term commitment. It wouldn't be fair." He fell silent, clearly surprised by his openness about something so deeply personal to him.

Chloe concentrated on keeping her breathing regular, her eyes following his movements as he withdrew his hand and once again sat back in his chair. He was obviously trying to warn her off, to let her know he wasn't interested. Well, he didn't need to bother himself on that score. She wasn't interested in him either, in any man, for that matter. The heavy weight of disappointment settling in her stomach was simply due to the fact she had obviously not made her feelings—or lack of them—clear enough.

"You can relax, Luke Warwick. I'm not going to fall in love with you," she said lightly after a moment's pause, her eyes suddenly sparkling with laugher. "But, you know, you're getting pretty long in the tooth to be putting it off for much longer. You don't want to miss the boat."

He raised his eyebrows, and laughed softly. "Thanks for your vote of confidence, Miss MacGregor. I'll bear that in mind."

"Good." She looked up at him with a sudden grin. "Well, to say we only met two days ago, I think I've disrupted your life pretty well so far, don't you? One minor rescue from an ex, and one major rescue from certain death."

His answering smile was immediate. "It certainly wasn't what I expected to happen when a colleague suggested I attend the ball, that's for sure."

"Why, what were you expecting?"

"Well, I got in touch with Clive, and he said Lucie was bringing a friend so it would make up the numbers. He mentioned that you'd split up from your boyfriend a while ago and still hadn't gotten over it yet." He held up his hand when she bridled and opened her mouth to protest.

"He didn't go into any details, and I didn't ask." Luke gave a half smile. "But I couldn't believe my eyes when I saw you walking into the room with Lucie— beautiful, cool and confident, and looking very much as if you couldn't give a damn about your ex. Best of all, you were the girl I'd seen collecting shells on the beach."

"You'd seen me?" Chloe blinked in surprise.

"Yes, a couple of times," he said slowly. "I'd—"

The telephone interrupted sharply, making them both jump, and Luke took his time getting up to answer it. His face lit up as he recognised the caller.

"Hey! How are you? I was going to call you later."

It was obviously a personal call, and Chloe immediately picked up her mug and wandered outside to give him some privacy. Walking down the side of the cottage, she found a weathered wooden bench placed close to the wall, looking out onto the pretty garden. This side of the cottage was sheltered from the wind, and she sat down, resting her head against the cool, stone walls and closing her eyes against the morning sun.

"There you are." Luke's soft gravelly voice made her start. "For a minute there, I thought you'd run away again."

She squinted up at him, shading her eyes from the sun with her hand. "You were on the phone; I didn't want to intrude. I hope you didn't cut the call short on my account."

"It's okay, I'll call her back later," he said easily, unaware of the sinking feeling that filled Chloe at his use of the word *her*. He joined her on the bench.

"You've got a lovely garden." She tried desperately to keep her breathing under control when his arm brushed hers, and she caught the faint trace of his aftershave.

"It needs a bit of work, I'm afraid." He frowned. "And it's not going to get done anytime soon, that's the problem. I'm in the middle of something pretty big at work which isn't leaving me much time for anything."

She nodded and bit her lip, hesitating before getting to her feet. "Well, I guess I'd better get going."

He stood quickly, reaching out to touch her arm. "I wasn't suggesting you should leave."

"Oh, I know you weren't," she smiled. "But I've

caused you more than enough trouble already and, besides, I really should be getting home."

"If you're sure, I'll run you home."

"Really, there's no need. I can—"

"I'll run you home." His tone brooked no argument. "Besides, you've no shoes."

****

The door to her cottage stood open as they pulled up outside, just as she had left it in her hurried exit last night. Despite her protestations, Luke insisted on giving the house a once-over, in case any opportunistic burglars had taken advantage of the empty property. Jasper trailed after him with interest. Leaving them both to it with a rueful shake of her head, Chloe quickly mopped up the rainwater that had blown in through the open door. Fortunately, the wind had been blowing in the opposite direction and the water was easily mopped up from the varnished floorboards; no real damage done.

She was putting the mop away when Luke reappeared to announce the house was safe. He smiled at her exaggerated sigh of relief, and hovered in the doorway for a moment as if he wanted to say more. In the end, he simply nodded his head and turned to leave, ducking his head under the doorframe as he left. "I'll leave you to it then."

She followed him to the door. Thank you again for everything."

"Anytime." He was walking to his car when he stopped suddenly. "Wait, I almost forgot…"

He jogged back to hand her a piece of paper. "My number. In case you ever decide to go storm walking again."

Chloe closed the door and leaned back against it, staring thoughtfully at the small scrap of paper in her hand. She pulled a face at the annoying voice in her head, the one telling her not to read anything into him leaving her his number, and went through to the kitchen. Flicking on the kettle, she opened the door to allow Jasper free run of the back garden.

The bright morning sun shone through the living room windows as she walked through with her mug of coffee, and she opened them to prevent the room from becoming too warm. Lighting two of her favourite scented candles, Chloe settled down in the chair closest to the window where she had a spectacular view across her garden, and over the cliff-tops to where the majestic ruins of Whitby Abbey stood in the distance, just as they had for centuries.

Catching sight of her mobile phone on the side table, left there since last night, she reached across to pick it up, running her finger lightly over the touchscreen to see if there were any missed calls or messages. Two missed calls—both from her mother—and one text from Rebekah. She had thought there might be a text from Lucie after Friday night's debacle, but there was nothing.

Why would Lucie set her up like that? Chloe sipped at her coffee, wondering at her friend's motivation. Well, it was definitely not a friendship worth maintaining.

She opened the text from Rebekah, smiling as she read the message.

Hi Sweetie, just a quick text to check you're ok after that horrendous storm last night? Thought about you up there on top of the world, braving the elements!

Should catch up soon for vino and nibbles. Love ya. X

Braving the elements—if only her friend knew how true that had been. She sent a short text back to say she was fine and suggested a couple of dates for them to meet up, before taking a deep breath and dialling her mother's telephone number. It was answered on the second ring.

"Hi Mum, it's me."

"Chloe, darling, I've been ringing you. Where on earth have you been?"

"Sorry, Mum, I didn't realise my phone was out of charge; I've only just picked up your missed calls." There was no way she would be telling her mother she had spent the night at Luke's cottage.

"But what about last night? I was calling your landline, and you didn't answer then either. I've been so worried."

"I'm sorry, I didn't mean to worry you. There was a huge storm last night and I didn't hear it ring. Maybe the lines were down."

"Oh. We didn't have a storm here." Her mother lived further inland, in a small village about half an hour's drive from her daughter. "Not a drop of rain."

"Well, good for you." She couldn't help laughing. "But that didn't stop the storm from raging over here."

"Well, as long as you're sure you're all right." Apparently convinced all was well, her mother went on to tell her the latest news from the village. Old Mrs. Bates had died, not that Chloe had ever heard of her, and her son had moved into his mother's house along with a much younger woman. Scandalous.

"Anyway, dear, have you any news?" Her mother eventually asked after half an hour.

"Oh, not really. It's all been rather quiet." Not quite the whole truth, considering what had happened over the last forty-eight hours, but Chloe couldn't face the over-reaction she knew would follow if she told her mother. Even so, Luke was forefront in her mind, and she was unable to not mention him at all. "Except that I've got a new neighbour. Someone has moved into Fulmar Cottage, across the beach. Do you remember it?"

"Yes, of course." Her mother was immediately interested in any potential gossip. "What are they like? Have you met them?

Too late, she realised her mistake, but there was no going back. "Well, I've only met the one person; I don't think it's a family who have moved in but…er…well, it's a…a man. I think he's on his own."

There had been nothing in his cottage to suggest he had a family, certainly there were no photographs of children or toys around. That wasn't to say he didn't have a casual girlfriend tucked away somewhere. There had been that phone call, though, she remembered with a sinking feeling. He had seemed so happy to hear *her* voice on the other end of the line.

"A man?" The sharp tone of her mother's voice broke into her thoughts. "What kind of man?"

She sighed. Why had she opened her big mouth? "What kind of man do you think? Of the male variety."

"There's no need to be sarcastic, Chloe MacGregor. You know exactly what I mean."

"He's a man, Mum," she drew in a deep breath, attempting to bite back her exasperation. "He's youngish, mid-thirties maybe. Professional, I think, but I've hardly spoken to him, so I don't know much. He seems nice."

There was a long pause. "Now, you're not going to get any foolish ideas, are you, love?"

"Oh Mum, please don't start." She closed her eyes and ran a weary hand over her face. "He's just someone who has moved into the cottage. I don't know him, and I probably won't get to know him. I can't imagine we would ever bump into each other."

"They're all the same, you know," her mother carried on. "They're all only interested in one thing; you can't trust any of them."

Chloe had listened to the same words many times over the years and she had never thought to challenge her mother before. But now Luke's words rang in her head. *Just because you haven't experienced it, doesn't mean that it can't exist, does it?*

"They're not all the same, Mum," she said softly. "Not all of them. Look at Sean and Rebekah. They're happy, and he would never look twice at another woman."

"Rubbish," her mother replied crisply. "He's very good at covering his tracks, that's all."

"No, you're wrong. Not Sean. Not ever."

"Well!" She was clearly surprised at her daughter's vehement response. "That may be so, but it's certainly the case for the majority. And besides, we're not the type of women the good men want. I'm afraid we don't have what they need. It's far better to leave well alone. You know that. Leave well alone."

"Yes, Mum," she whispered, unable to deny her mother's logic when she knew it to be true.

"Oh Chloe, I'm only thinking of you, my darling," her mother said quietly. "You know I'm right, don't you? Look at what you went through with Chris. I don't want you to get hurt again."

"I know." Chloe stared through the window.

"Look, let's forget about that silly neighbour of yours. He's nothing to do with us, is he?"

"No, Mum."

They exchanged a few more pleasantries before her mother eventually hung up the phone, promising to call her the next day.

Chloe tossed the phone on the table and leaned back in her chair, staring at nothing, consumed by the hollow feeling in the pit of her stomach. She stirred when Jasper wandered in from the garden.

"She's right, you know, Jasper," she said, reaching into her jeans pocket and withdrawing the now-crumpled piece of paper with Luke's mobile number written on it.

"See this?" She wafted it in front of Jasper's nose. "He didn't ask for my number, did he? Obviously, didn't have any inclination to contact me himself. Just gave me his number, to ring him in case of emergencies."

She crumpled up the scrap of paper and threw it into the wastepaper bin by the fire. "I don't need rescuing."

As she walked through to the little sitting room at the back of the cottage, her gloomy mood lifted. She loved this room; her workroom. All her jewellery-making tools and materials were stored in here, and the view from her workbench—facing the window—was a constant source of inspiration. She turned to Jasper with a smile.

"Well, maybe I needed rescuing last night, but that was a one-off, and one that I don't intend to repeat. So, you'd better not make me."

Chapter Three

"I told my Harry the weather would be fine."
Maureen Clifford gave a satisfied smile. "We needed
that storm last weekend to pave the way for all this
sun."

The day had dawned bright and sunny for the
annual village gala and, behind Maureen's bright smile,
Chloe recognised the relief felt by the woman who had
spent the last six months painstakingly organising the
event. She had been coaxing local businesses, and the
local Cub-Scout and Brownie groups, into decorating
the trailers which would parade through the village,
kindly lent to them for the day by nearby farmers and
landowners. Her efforts had been rewarded by a
procession of eleven brightly decorated floats that were
unrecognisable from their humble origins.

"You've done an amazing job, Maureen, you really
have," said Chloe, as she made a few last-minute
adjustments to her own jewellery stall.

"Oh, thank you, my dear, it's become a bit of a
habit, really. I don't know what I'd do with myself if I
didn't have this to organise every year." Maureen's
eyes suddenly widened, and she pursed her lips in
disapproval. "What on earth is William doing setting up
his stall over there? I purposely gave him the plot next
to Carol's butterfly buns. Excuse me, Chloe dear, I'll

have to have a word…William!" She hurried off with a determined step.

"Uh-oh, I think William is in for a bit of a telling off, Jasper." Chloe smiled down at the dog sitting obediently by her folding chair. Considering that Jasper spent most of her time without a leash, not needing one on their own private beach, the dog had happily accepted the inconvenience of having to wear one while Chloe took part in the gala. It was one of the many rules that seemed to increase year on year as a result of the ever-growing health and safety regulations.

Adeptly sidestepping the large stick of candy floss being waved enthusiastically by an over-excited young boy, she retreated behind her stall, smoothing her hands quickly over her blouse. While the white, gypsy-style skirt and matching top were cool and pretty, it was perhaps not the best choice of colour for taking part in an event full of small children and numerous food stalls. Never mind, she would be safe enough behind her own stall.

As the sun rose higher in the cloudless sky, it beat down with an intensity she could feel across her shoulders, the heat accentuating the weight of the long plait that hung down her back. Thank goodness she had remembered to use sunscreen this morning before setting off. Anticipating a long day beneath the sun, she had brought a wide-brimmed straw hat with her, and she put it on now as she perched on her seat, casting a last-minute glance across her display as people began wandering happily along the various stalls selling everything from handmade crafts, to pot plants, to general bric-a-brac. Across the way, Maureen was having a quiet but nonetheless heated debate with

William over his renegade stall, and Chloe couldn't help but laugh.

Reaching into her shoulder bag, she withdrew a small paper bag containing pieces of her favourite sweet, Edinburgh rock. Nibbling absently on a pink nugget, she enjoyed a spot of people-watching while she sat behind her stall and made the most of the lovely summer day. Almost without realising it, her gaze scanned the crowd, that familiar feeling in the pit of her stomach telling her she was unconsciously searching for Chris, that she didn't believe he would leave her alone now he had made contact again.

She sighed in anger and frustration, flexing her shoulders to ease her tension. *Why was she even thinking about him?* That was exactly what he wanted. He had obviously deliberately engineered their meeting at the Ball, and was probably now sitting back and laughing, knowing she would be looking over her shoulder every minute. Well, she would not give him the satisfaction, whether he knew it or not. She would not let him win.

Fortunately, as more and more people arrived, Chloe found she was kept busy with a steady stream of customers, and all thoughts of Chris were pushed to the back of her mind. She was in her element, helping customers choose the right piece of jewellery to match what they were looking for.

"I love your ring." A young woman pointed to the large, polished amethyst set in a wide silver band, and which Chloe wore on her right hand.

"Oh, thank you." Chloe smiled and held out her hand for the girl to take a closer look. "I make them myself. If it's the setting you like, there's one here with a moonstone instead of the amethyst."

She reached across to gently ease the ring she referred to from where it nestled in a black velvet cushion. "It's quite a small size so should be fine for your lovely, slim fingers. Here, try it on."

The girl slid it over her middle finger, but it stopped halfway down, and she withdrew it to try slipping it onto her ring finger. After a slight pause, it eased over her knuckle and she held out her hand to consider the effect.

"It looks lovely." Chloe nodded and smiled. "Although, if you would prefer one for your middle finger, I can have a look in my stock to see if I've got something similar that's the next size up?"

The girl considered the ring for a few seconds before eventually shaking her head. "No. I think I like it on that finger. It's a little larger and heavier than I usually wear, but I like it. I was looking at all the rings you wear and think they look really nice. I wish I had the confidence to wear them like you do, but I think I'll start off with just the one."

"Oh, thank you! What a lovely thing to say." She reached across and handed her the empty ring box. "Are you going to keep it on?" The girl nodded.

After paying for her purchase, the girl moved away, still admiring the ring on her finger, and Chloe heaved a surreptitious sigh of relief when there were no other customers waiting. It was mid-afternoon, and she had been busy non-stop since eleven o'clock that morning. Taking advantage of the lull, she decided to replenish her display from the stock she had stored in a box under the table.

"It looks like you've had a successful afternoon."

She recognised the soft, gravelly voice immediately, and took a moment to compose herself before straightening up and turning towards Luke. Despite the heat, he looked cool and relaxed in black jeans and a grey marl t-shirt, worn tight enough to emphasize his muscular chest and arms.

Trying hard not to stare as she recalled how those very same arms had drawn her close against him, she managed to lift her gaze to meet his pale green eyes.

"Hello." She smiled as if her heart wasn't racing. "Yes, it's been quite busy."

He nodded, and gestured towards her hands. "I saw you had a bit of a thing for jewellery, but it didn't occur to me that you actually made it yourself." He paused briefly and shot her an enquiring glance. "I take it you do make it?"

"Yes. All made by my own fair hands."

He stepped closer to admire the beautifully crafted jewellery. "It's pretty amazing stuff. You're very talented, Chloe MacGregor; clearly a woman with hidden depths."

Unused to such genuine praise, she could feel the colour rising in her cheeks, making her even more uncomfortable in the heat, and she busied herself arranging the new stock on the table. "Thank you."

"Have you had a look round at the other stalls yet?"

Relieved to be on safer ground, she shook her head. "No, I haven't had a chance yet."

"Are you allowed a break?" He looked across to the woman sitting behind the next stall, the top of which was crammed full of what appeared to be hand-knitted toys.

Betty looked up and immediately recognised her cue. "Oh, Chloe, of course. You've never stopped. You take a break and spend some time with your young man here. I'll watch your stall for you."

"Oh, he's not—"

"Thank you very much. That's very kind." Luke bent down to untie Jasper's lead from the chair leg and ushered Chloe from the stall.

Uncomfortably aware of Betty's curious gaze upon them, and completely at a loss as to what to say to Luke, Chloe made her way quickly to the next stall, feigning interest in the eclectic mix of wares covering the local Brownie group's table.

"Fifty pence a go?" The Brownie looked at them hopefully, her small round face hot and sweaty but nonetheless shining with enthusiasm. She waved her hand towards the shallow wooden box half filled with sand, into which rows of lollipop sticks had been placed at regular intervals.

"Hmm, what do I have to do?"

"You have to pick a lollipop stick. If you pick one that has a gold star on the bottom, you win a prize."

"Oh, right." Chloe nodded her head seriously. "And what prize do I get?"

"Well, you get to choose any of the stuff on the table." The girl waved her hand across the table as if it held a display of fabulously glittering giftware. In actual fact, the prizes consisted of several boxes of unopened perfume, packets of chocolate (which looked suspiciously as though they had melted), and various bottles of bubble bath.

"Ok, I'll have two, please." She handed over a one-pound coin and leaned over the line of sticks, nibbling thoughtfully on a fresh piece of rock. "Hmm, I think I'll go for that one." She reached towards a slightly crooked stick standing further apart from the rest.

"Really? You think that's a winning lollipop stick?" Luke's voice was close in her ear.

"You don't think that's a good choice?" She pretended to reconsider her options. "Which one would you go for then?"

He leaned closer, his shoulder brushing against her as he did so, and causing a tingling sensation along her spine. "Hmm, I think that one has a winning look about it, don't you?"

"Go on, then," she nudged him. "I paid for two sticks—you pick that one and I'll stick with my original, lopsided one."

She stood back and folded her arms across her chest, watching as he winked at the Brownie waiting patiently for them to play the game. When he withdrew his chosen stick, bereft of the necessary star, Chloe was unable to prevent the short burst of laughter escaping her lips and she clapped her hands together gleefully.

"Really?" His lips twitched, as if he were trying to maintain a hurt expression at her obvious delight.

It was with a certain sense of satisfaction that she plucked the lollipop stick she had chosen from the sand and revealed a shiny, golden star stuck to the bottom. Luke turned away with a groan. "I should have known better."

"Ha! Serves you right, Luke Warwick. You should have listened to me." She favoured him with a smug smile before turning to the young girl. "Ooh, can I choose a prize now?"

After some deliberation, she eventually chose a

bottle of Tahitian Paradise bubble bath; one that promised to transport her every future bathing experience into a tropical adventure.

Triumphantly holding her prize, her earlier discomfort faded as Luke fell into step beside her, and together they wandered slowly along the line of stalls. They paused occasionally to look more closely at the various objects for sale, or to allow Jasper to explore the myriad of scents that assailed her canine sense of smell.

"So, how's the shoulder?"

"Oh, it's not too bad; hurts a little if I catch it." Chloe shrugged and pulled a face, her actions belying her words.

"I'm not surprised. It was quite a nasty cut." He nodded, turning his head to look at her with a half-smile. "It was some night."

His gaze held hers and time seemed to slow, the sounds of the gala fading into the distance as if they were walking in a vacuum. Swallowing against a suddenly dry throat, her voice came out as a whisper. "Yes. It was."

Was he, too, remembering the closeness they had shared? That kiss?

"Hard to believe such a difference in the weather," he carried on, apparently unaware of her discomposure and clearly not thinking at all about that kiss.

"I know, it's so hot," she managed after a pause, relieved to find she at least sounded relatively compos mentis, even if she didn't feel it. "I think I'm going to melt."

"Well, we've just about covered the gala, so what do you say to a tall glass of ice-cold lemonade at the

Ship Inn when you finish?" He glanced around at the thinning crowds. "Or perhaps a G&T, poured over ice and lemon? They have a beer garden, so there would be no problem with Jasper."

Desperately thirsty and longing to find some shade, her response was immediate. "I'd like that."

****

Luke paused in the doorway, a glass of lemonade in each hand, and a bottle of mineral water tucked under his arm. Chloe was already sitting at a table under the shady canopy of an old tree, its branches providing welcome relief from the relentless heat of the sun. Underneath the table, Jasper was panting hard as she, too, struggled with the heat. Unaware of his gaze, Chloe reached into her bag and pulled out the bubble bath, flicking open the lid and raising it to her nose to breathe in the fragrance. Judging by her smile it was obviously not that bad, and he felt an unfamiliar lurch in his stomach. She was unlike anyone he'd spent time with before. There was a gentle innocence, a *goodness* about her and, despite his better judgement, he wanted to get to know her better.

As he made his way across the courtyard, she bent forward to drop the bottle into her bag. A further smile playing across her lips as she withdrew a small piece of pale green rock and slipped it into her mouth.

"Are you hungry?"

She jumped slightly and looked up. "No, no…it's a piece of rock." After a brief hesitation, she reached once more into her bag to withdraw the white paper bag. "Would you like one?"

He set the glasses on the table and retrieved a small plastic container from underneath the table, filling it with the bottled water for Jasper, and smiling in amusement as he did so. "Offered with such enthusiasm! I take it you're rather partial to…what is it, anyway?" He peered into the bag.

"Edinburgh rock. Have you ever tried it?"

"Can't say I have." He shook his head. "Thanks for the offer, but no, I'm not really a sweet sort of a guy."

"Don't be so hard on yourself." She teased. "I can imagine there are some people who might think you're sweet."

He rewarded her with the sardonic smile she deserved.

She gave a sudden yawn and quickly covered her mouth with her hand, her cheeks flooding with colour. "Oh gosh, excuse me. I'm so sorry."

He gave a wide grin. "Perhaps it's me who ought to be sorry. I'm clearly boring you."

Chloe stiffened and shook her head immediately, a frown marring her brow. "Oh no, of course not. You're not boring at all. It must be the heat and…and I haven't slept too well over the last couple of nights…"

His heart gave a solid thump, an acknowledgement that something wasn't right. Her conciliatory tone and wary glance were at odds with their otherwise light and playful exchanges.

Did she really think he had been serious?

He leaned forward to lightly touch her arm. "Hey, I was joking."

She blinked and then nodded, dropping her gaze for a moment as she fiddled with one of her rings. She looked up with a quick smile. "Of course, you were. I guess I'm not always that good at reading people. Sorry." She gave a laugh and shrugged, her smile widening once more. "They have a standing joke in the office at work, trying to out-do themselves with whoever can come up with the wildest thing they can think of that I'll believe."

"You work in an office? I thought you made jewellery."

"I do, but only in my spare time. One day, though, I'd like to do it full-time. If I can sell enough, that is."

She appeared relaxed once more and, although the knot of worry in his chest subsided, he remained uneasy, as if he were missing something important. "What is it that's been keeping you awake at night, then?"

"Oh, nothing major. Just work stuff." She waved her hand dismissively. "I won't bore you."

"You sure? I'm a good listener. A problem shared and all that."

She wrinkled her nose prettily and gave a sigh. "It's just been an odd sort of a week."

He leaned back in his chair, waiting for her to gather her thoughts. He felt again that unusual pull, that feeling of wanting to know her, protect her, to do anything to prevent that odd, vulnerable expression darken her eyes.

"John, the guy that I work for is one of the directors in the company, and he came in on Monday and told us he's taking early retirement, with immediate effect." She gave a quiet laugh, spreading her hands and shaking her head in obvious confusion. "It's completely out of the blue; never mentioned it before now. I've worked with him for five years, so I thought we were pretty close. And then, Mary, the PA I share an office with, also handed in her notice." She paused for a moment and reached forward for her lemonade, taking a long swallow before reaching once more into her bag for another piece of rock and nibbling on it thoughtfully.

Luke shifted in his chair. "Do you think there's something going on between them?"

"Oh no, nothing like that. I mean, it was a bit weird but, you know, I guess it happens." She gestured with the sweet in her hand before continuing. "But then, the next day, the MD called everyone into a full staff meeting and told us that the company has been bought out, taken over, whatever you want to call it. Again, it was so out of the blue. No rumours, no inkling of any sort of trouble or anything. We've been told that it shouldn't mean job losses, but…well, who knows?"

Luke drew in a long breath, his eyes fixed on her face, unable to quite believe it. It had to be a coincidence. He took a quick sip of his drink, aware that his mouth was suddenly dry. Chloe appeared lost in her own musing as she popped the rock into her mouth and sighed, clearly unaware of his own racing thoughts.

"It makes me wonder, with John leaving so suddenly, does it mean things are really bad and he's jumping ship?" She shook her head with a smile. "Excuse the pun."

He stared at her, careful to keep his face impassive, and she quickly added, "Sorry, I forgot to say; I work for a shipbuilding company…hence the bit about the pun. Anyway, I don't think John would leave us in the lurch if things were bad. He's been there from the start, and I'm sure he'd stay and see things through. Like I said, it's all a little unsettling."

She looked at him, obviously expecting some sort

of response.

In Luke's mind, there could really be no doubt, but he forced a smile and asked the question anyway.

"Who did you say you worked for?"

"Hardaker Shipbuilding Ltd."

Despite knowing the answer before she had spoken, his heart thumped against his chest on hearing it confirmed. He nodded slowly, taking another long sip of his drink to buy himself some time. "And do you think your boss...John, did you say? Do you think John's sudden decision to retire, and the buyout of the company are related?"

"I don't know." She pulled a face. "My gut reaction says not, but I can't think why he would retire so suddenly. I was worried it might be ill-health; either himself or his wife, but he said they're both fine. He told me not to worry, but I can't help it. Something's not right." She gave a helpless shrug. "Anyway, because the company has been bought out, they're not going to recruit to Mary's post immediately, and I've been asked to cover for her until the new owners decide what they want to do."

"I guess as PA to one of the directors, you'll be privy to a good deal of the strategic decisions being made." He kept his voice neutral. "So, what does your 'gut reaction' tell you? Knowing what you know now, were there any clues or signs that things weren't going so well?"

She leaned back in her chair, one hand absently twisting the long plait hanging over her shoulder. "I don't know," she answered thoughtfully, after a pause.

"We're well known for the quality of our workmanship; that hasn't changed, we still get fantastic feedback. I know John was concerned that profit margins were smaller than he expected. There were quite a few heated discussions with Niall, our finance director." She gave another shrug. "But that's nothing new. Niall's really experienced, seems to know what he's doing, and was happy that the budgets and profits reflected the current financial market." She gave a wry smile. "He threw it right back at John; told him he needed to work on bringing in more business if he was that concerned about it."

About to question her further, Luke paused. This wasn't fair, or ethical. He leaned forward, resisting the urge to brush a stray strand of hair from her cheek. "I can see why you've been having difficulty sleeping. It's an unsettling time."

She nodded unhappily, before straightening up and smiling brightly. "Anyway, enough about my work stuff. What about you? What do you do?"

He sat back immediately. *What to say?* "I um…I run my own company."

She waited for him to continue, raising her eyebrows when he didn't speak.

"Doing…?"

He gave a soft laugh. He deserved that. "Mainly consultancy; basically, companies ask us to come in and troubleshoot. We work with the company to identify the issues and areas for development, and offer advice on how to overcome any difficulties." He shrugged. "I set the company up ten years ago with a five-thousand-pound loan from my grandfather and what I suppose was a bit of a cocky attitude. It took me three years and several lessons learned to make a profit and lose the attitude…or some of it, at least. But I paid him back, and seven years on, we're doing pretty well."

"Sounds like maybe the MD should have asked you to come in and troubleshoot our company."

Her smile faded when Luke's only response was a blank stare. *Many a true word spoken in jest.* He reached down to scratch behind Jasper's ears.

"You never did tell me why your very ladylike dog has a boy's name."

"Oh. Well, she already had a name when I bought her." She blinked at the abrupt change of subject, but recovered quickly. "I got her from a family in the village and the little boy there had named all the pups, irrespective of whether they were male or female. Jasper was his favourite, and I had to promise to bring her round to see him every now and then, so I thought I'd better keep the name he gave her. Jasper doesn't seem to mind one way or the other, though, obviously."

The frequent use of her name had the dog looking up at Chloe enquiringly, her ears pricking up as the village church clock chimed four.

"Four o'clock, Jasper." She leaned down to pat her dog, with a grimace. "I suppose we really ought to make our way to see Mum."

"You make that sound like a chore." Luke smiled, getting to his feet as Chloe pushed her chair back.

"You haven't met my mother."

He watched them leave, and sank into his chair with a long sigh, unable to believe this new twist of fate. He had deliberately stayed away from the beach all week, deliberately kept his gaze averted whenever he passed the point on his driveway that afforded a view of Chloe's cliff path. Get yourself down to the gala, he'd told himself this morning. Get involved in village life, be a part of the community.

Had he secretly been hoping to bump into Chloe? Probably, if he were being truthful.

But this? This was too much.

In an instant, his life had suddenly become way too complicated.

****

Niall Jefferson gestured to the empty chair placed directly in front of the large desk, before taking his own seat and leaning back.

"Well, Chloe, I wanted to have a few minutes with you before the new MD arrives. With John and Mary leaving at this crucial time, we're going to have to rally around and pull together. I know we've not worked with each other directly, but John always spoke very highly of you, and I wanted you to know I'm looking forward to working with you."

Chloe nodded, but remained silent. She had never been particularly fond of Niall; she'd always thought him arrogant and full of his own self-importance. As the finance director, he obviously carried a great deal of responsibility, but there was something about him that made her uncomfortable. Mary, who had been PA to both Jeff Hardaker—the departing MD—and Niall, had not seemed to notice his sometimes condescending manner towards her. Or, if she had noticed, she had chosen to ignore it.

It was going to be strange in the office now. While Mary's constant chatter had often irritated her, the two women had got on well despite the thirty-year difference in age.

Niall shifted in his chair, straightening his waistcoat beneath the black, pin-striped suit jacket as he did so. Sunlight streamed in through the large picture window behind him, throwing him into silhouette and hiding his expression.

"You shared an office with Mary for a number of years." It was a statement rather than a question and, again, Chloe remained silent. "You always seemed to get on well together; I never heard otherwise..." His voice trailed off in an uncharacteristically hesitant manner before he again shifted in his chair and cleared his throat.

"What I mean to say is that Mary's decision to leave...well, it was rather sudden." He paused and leaned forward slightly. His expression was suddenly visible, his eyes narrowed assessingly. "Before she left, did Mary discuss her reasons for leaving with you?"

She was momentarily thrown, uncomfortably aware that he was tensed for her response. "Um...no not really. It was a complete surprise if I'm being honest. She had never spoken of retiring so soon." Chloe shrugged. "She just said she'd talked it over with her husband, and they had decided they were financially secure enough for her to retire. From what she said, she fancied spending some time pottering around in the garden."

She smiled uncertainly. She couldn't argue with Mary's reasoning, but still wondered why it had never been mentioned before.

Niall relaxed back into his chair, the tension visibly easing as he ran a casual hand through the thick, brown hair beginning to grey at the temples. He looked younger than his fifty years, and his hair was naturally wavy—a fact he attempted to disguise by keeping it short and waxing it to within an inch of its life.

I hope he wipes his hands before meeting the new MD, she thought distractedly. *His hand must be covered in grease.*

"Yes, we have perhaps been guilty of forgetting that she's not in the first flush of youth anymore," he said now, bringing her attention back to the conversation. "I have noticed a change in her over the last few months, a certain weariness. Have you not?"

She returned his direct gaze without flinching. "Actually, no, I can't say I have. But then you worked with her far more than I did."

"Yes, of course." He appeared to consider their conversation for a moment before sitting up straight in his chair. "So, back to business. As you are aware, neither John nor Mary are being replaced in the short term; that will be a decision for the new MD. Until that time, you and I are going to have our work cut out."

When she nodded her understanding, he carried on in a serious tone. "Unfortunately, the other directors appeared not to heed my advice, and I was outvoted in terms of the buyout which, as finance director, I find particularly galling. It makes me concerned about ulterior motives. I have no idea what the plans are for the company and, if I don't know what the plans are, I am not able to undertake financial planning effectively."

He swivelled his chair towards the window, staring thoughtfully across the busy boat yard and dry dock below. "I need eyes and ears, Chloe. Eyes and ears. We need to watch each other's back, because I for one do not believe this *no job losses* crap! If the finance director is not involved in future planning, then he's not the finance director, is he? And if I go, you can bet your bottom dollar I'll take a few people with me."

For a moment, Chloe was speechless and could only stare at the back of his head. Despite the seriousness of his words—or perhaps because of them—she wondered, rather incongruously, if he was trying to see how many times he could use the words 'finance director' in two minutes. She blinked as his chair turned back to her in a sudden movement.

"Can I trust you, Chloe?"

"Yes, of course."

"Good, good. Then I'll say no more, but I think it was important for you to know where I stand. Where *we* stand." Once again, he seemed to relax, and he smiled. "I apologise if I was overly blunt, but I want to impress upon you that I have doubts that everything is what it seems. We need to keep our wits about us, yes?"

He gazed at her fiercely for a moment, before swivelling his chair back to face the window, clearly signalling the end of their conversation.

****

Chloe pulled the door to Niall's office closed behind her and turned slowly towards her desk, but made no move towards it. She could feel a dull ache across her shoulders, and she shrugged them up to her ears to ease the tension pulling across her spine; what a surreal conversation that had been.

Her eyes strayed from the door to the clock hanging on the opposite wall, and wondered what time the new MD would be making an appearance. She gazed around the office critically, trying to see it from a stranger's perspective. Floor to ceiling windows filled the right-hand side of the room, allowing for a striking view of the boat yard, harbour, and sea beyond. In front of the window nearest to the corridor was a small, round coffee table with matching easy chairs for use by any visitors waiting to see the directors. The wall behind her contained two doors—one leading to Niall's office, the other to John's—with desks for both herself and Mary placed to one side of each door. The placement of the desks lent a pleasing symmetry to the airy office. A further door on the left-hand wall led into the meeting room, and a photocopier and several filing cabinets took up the remaining space in one corner. No sounds of the busy boat yard below filtered through the windows, and the ambience was one of calm and quiet; not a bad first impression.

No sooner had this thought entered her head than the intrusive peal of the telephone on her desk made her jump, and she snatched it up quickly. After a brief conversation, she transferred the caller to Niall before taking her seat, automatically unlocking her laptop, and calling up her emails. Within minutes, the familiarity of her daily routine relieved the tension, and calmed the butterflies in her stomach, but Niall's words occupied her thoughts.

Could he possibly be right in his mistrust of the new regime, or was it simply sour grapes because he had not been involved? Normally, she was not given to paranoia, but the fact that both John and Mary had left so suddenly was odd. Perhaps there was some truth in Niall's words.

I wish Luke were here.

The thought came unbidden, and she blinked in surprise. Where on earth had that come from? She thought of the way his pale green eyes caught hers, the way one corner of his mouth turned up when he smiled reluctantly, and was unnerved by a wave of something akin to homesickness settling over her. Luke radiated strength and confidence and, feeling as unsettled as she did this morning, she wished he were here to tell her that everything would be all right.

The butterflies returned to her stomach, although this time for a different reason, and she frowned, shaking her head as if to negate the knowledge that he was featuring in her thoughts far too often. Going down that road would only lead to disappointment on both sides.

She shook her head impatiently, pushing away thoughts of him with some difficulty. Right now wasn't the time to worry about that. Straightening her shoulders and lifting her chin resolutely, she made herself a coffee and, with a fresh packet of rock sitting on her desk, forced herself to concentrate on pulling together the reports Niall had indicated he might need for the meeting this morning.

An hour later, while searching for a folder in one of the filing cabinets, Chloe heard Jeff Hardaker's familiar voice outside in the corridor. She took a steadying breath, closed the cabinet drawer, and turned to meet the two men as they walked into the office.

Her welcoming smile froze on her lips as Jeff turned to introduce the man standing beside him. She gazed straight into familiar pale green eyes.

Luke.

Chapter Four

"Chloe, I'd like you to meet Luke Warwick, owner and founder of the Warwick Company Ltd, and the new managing director of Hardaker Shipbuilding Ltd." Jeff Hardaker beamed, completely oblivious to her dazed surprise. "Luke, this is Chloe MacGregor, one of the best assistants we have. As I mentioned, following Mary's retirement, Chloe has agreed to step into the breach and will be your office and administrative support in the first instance. Any information you need, she will have it at her fingertips, I'm sure."

"Actually, we've already met," said Luke smoothly, moving forward to shake her ice-cold hand. "It's a pleasure to see you again, Miss MacGregor."

Struggling to maintain her composure, she forced herself to nod politely. "Mr. Warwick."

"Good, good. Is Niall in?" Jeff indicated the door opposite.

"Yes, of course." Relieved to find her voice sounded completely normal, she turned away from Luke's gaze. "He's expecting you."

Knocking on Niall's door before announcing their arrival, she deliberately avoided Luke's glance as she led them both in, before leaving and closing the door behind her.

For a moment, she simply stood by her desk, a

sense of the surreal stealing over her, but then sank slowly into her chair. Luke Warwick was the new MD. She couldn't believe it.

She chewed her lip, recalling his expression when he had taken her hand. He had shown no surprise, and it was clear he had expected to see her. She thought back to their conversation at the weekend and remembered how he had quickly changed the subject when she had shown an interest in his company.

The more she thought about it, the more her shock was gradually replaced by ice-cold anger at his deception. Did it go further than simply not telling her he was buying out the company where she worked? Had he deliberately sought her out in an attempt to get inside information?

Her mind when into overdrive. It was entirely possible that Clive had learnt of the buyout, and mentioned to Luke that coincidentally he knew someone who worked there. *How easy it would have been then for Luke to engineer a meeting with that person, perhaps for instance at a charity event?*

Stupid, stupid, stupid. When would she ever learn?

Feeling sick to the stomach at the thought of being used, she gave a hollow laugh at the situation she now found herself in. How ironic that, only a couple of hours ago, she was wishing Luke were here to make everything all right again.

She was such a fool.

A trip to the bathroom allowed Chloe to freshen up and reassure herself that there were no outward signs of her emotional turmoil. And when she took in a tray of coffee for them, she was fully composed once more.

It was more than an hour later when Jeff left the

office, informing her that Mr. Warwick would be spending the rest of the day with the finance director. As Niall called on her time and time again to bring in more reports or to explain certain figures, she was aware of Luke's gaze following her every movement, but she studiously ignored him.

The hands on the wall clock seemed to take forever to reach five o'clock, but when they did, she breathed a sigh of relief and knocked on Niall's door, entering at his request.

"Niall, if there's nothing else you need, I'll go home now."

"Yes, of course. Goodnight then, Chloe."

"Goodnight, Miss MacGregor." Luke waited until she finally met his glance and then smiled slightly, his expression unreadable. "Thank you for your help this afternoon; you've been extremely efficient."

"Goodnight, Mr. Warwick." She gave a curt nod as she turned and left the office.

****

The following morning, Chloe stepped out of her car and took a long, deep breath before lifting her chin, pasting on a bright smile, and walking briskly into the office building. Having spent the night tossing and turning, analysing every little nuance of the conversations she had shared with Luke, she remained convinced he had known exactly who she was and where she worked. Well, she was damned if she would let him know how much that hurt.

Despite her best intentions, her step faltered when she walked along the corridor to her office and saw him coming in the opposite direction.

"Chloe, good morning."

"Morning." She flashed him a breezy smile without slowing her pace, but was forced to stop when he caught her arm.

"Hey." He smiled, but his brow remained furrowed. "Look, I'm sorry about yesterday."

She deliberately looked down at his fingers resting lightly on her arm, waiting until he dropped his hand. "Really? What are you sorry about?"

"You seem angry with me. I guess it's because you think I knew you worked here. But I didn't."

She gave a soft laugh, not attempting to hide her disbelief. "Do you really think I'm stupid, Luke? You fully expected to see me yesterday, so don't insult me by lying about it."

"I'm not lying." He grimaced and gave a sigh. "Yes, I was expecting to see you yesterday, but only because you'd told me where you worked the day before, in the pub garden. I had no idea before then. I promise."

"So, why didn't you say anything at the time?"

"Because you threw me completely." He shrugged, shaking his head with a disarming smile. "It was the last thing I was expecting, and I was trying to process what that actually meant. And then you left, and the opportunity had gone. I'm sorry. I didn't intend to deceive you."

At a loss for words, she lowered her eyes from his searching gaze. He seemed sincere and entirely plausible, but did she believe him? Did it even matter if she believed him? What difference would it make? There was nothing between them, and there certainly couldn't be now that he was her boss. That thought brought a sudden, gut-wrenching ache, and she shook her head.

"It doesn't really matter one way or the other." She briefly met his gaze. "Let's just forget about it, shall we?"

She sounded half-hearted, even to her own ears, and Luke's expression remained troubled, but he nodded anyway.

"Well, I'll let you get on then."

As he moved past her, she saw Niall standing at the end of the corridor.

"Morning, Niall." Her smile faded when he continued to stare at her for a few seconds before turning and walking away, as if she hadn't spoken.

She stared at the empty space where he had been standing. What on earth was that about? She moved her shoulders uneasily. There was something about him; something she couldn't quite put her finger on. Biting her lip pensively, she made her way to her office and switched on the laptop. Life was certainly going to be different around here now.

****

The rest of the week passed without event, and Chloe saw little of Luke while he familiarised himself with the various departments of his new company. The corridors and staff rooms were full of girlish laughter, and conversations about the gorgeous new MD, discussions about whether or not he was married and, she noticed, a definite increase in heavy perfumes and shorter hemlines.

Relieved to have the office to herself, she carefully avoided engaging in any water-cooler discussions about Mr. Luke Warwick. She was wryly aware that she had experienced first-hand what those girls were fantasizing about, and knew exactly how it felt to have him kiss her, his hands expertly teasing a response from her body.

She might have found it more difficult to push aside such thoughts had Niall not been in a particularly foul mood since that first day with Luke. He spent the following days banging doors, slamming drawers into filing cabinets, and talking endlessly on the telephone, before finally stalking out of the office on Thursday and informing her that he had several important meetings with clients and would not be back until Monday.

By half past four on Friday night, she was more than ready to go home. With some relief, she finally switched off her laptop and left the office, looking forward to a few days away from her twitchy, snappy new boss.

*****

"You did what?"

Rebekah sat forward so abruptly that several large drops of wine spilled over her fingers and onto the multi-coloured throw. She was sitting cross-legged at one end of her sofa, with Chloe sitting likewise at the other, a large bowl of tortilla chips nestled between them, and a bottle of wine standing on the floor within easy reach. Jasper was curled up comfortably in front of the original tiled fireplace of the beautiful Victorian terraced cottage Rebekah shared with her husband, Sean. Chloe was updating her best friend on all that had happened since they had last seen each other, starting with the charity ball, and finishing by describing the dreadful storm and how she had spent the night in Luke's arms.

"It's not how it sounds..." she giggled at her

friend's expression.

"Oh my God, Chloe MacGregor!" Rebekah squealed, reaching for the tortilla chips. "You live like a…a…a virtual hermit for months, and then you casually tell me that you spent the night with a guy just two days after meeting him."

"You know, I could hear you two shrieking and cackling while I was in the shower." Sean walked into the living room, an easy grin lighting up his handsome face. "I'm glad I'm going out; I don't think my eardrums could take it. I'm surprised Jasper hasn't run for cover, poor dog."

"You won't believe what Chloe's just told me. She spent the night with some random guy who rescued her from certain death."

"Glad to hear it." His grin widened, and he leaned over the back of the sofa to drop a kiss on Chloe's reddened cheek. "About time you had some fun. You're far too gorgeous to sit on that shelf for ever."

He walked through to the kitchen to take a four-pack of cold beer from the fridge, before returning to give his wife a lingering kiss. "Well, I'll leave you ladies to it. Love you, Bek. I'll try not to be too late."

"So, where have you banished him to then?" Chloe turned back to her friend as Sean closed the door behind him.

"Oh, he's gone to watch the big game at one of his mates in the village." She reached for the bottle to refill their glasses. "So, come on, spill."

Ten minutes later, Rebekah sat back and looked at her with a smile. "Well, it's not a tale of wild, passionate sex, but God, it's so romantic."

"Well, it would be if I hadn't just found out that

he's going to be my boss. It's too much of a coincidence. What if he was using me?"

Her friend wrinkled her nose. "Who cares? You say he's good looking, sexy? Why don't you use him back? Use him for sex, hey?"

Chloe frowned in distaste. "I'm not into that. You know me, I'm not really into the whole 'sex" thing."

"That's because you haven't slept with anyone who can push the right buttons. I don't think it sounds as if this guy would have a problem there."

Her stomach quivered at the mere thought of Luke's kisses, and she met her friend's gaze. Rebekah gave a shout of laughter. "I thought so. Go on, have some fun for once." She became serious all of a sudden. "Not everyone is like Chris, you know. In fact, very few of them are. You can't let him win."

"I know." She smiled back. "I don't plan to."

Luke might know how to push her buttons, but it wouldn't take him long to realise that she was not able to reciprocate, that she was a failure in bed, would it? It wouldn't be fun for long, and then she would still have to work with him, see his contempt for her in his eyes.

"Working with him would make it awkward." She shook her head.

"Get another job."

"Oh, just like that?" She laughed at her friend's optimistic outlook. A bubbly, vivacious blonde who had a live-for-the-moment attitude for life, she sometimes envied Rebekah.

"Tell you what, let's Google this Luke Warwick to see if we can get a picture of him. If he's drop-dead gorgeous, then we'll discuss whether or not you need to be looking for a new job so you can get jiggy with him without any hassles at work."

Half a bottle of wine later, they were poring over Rebekah's laptop and had found numerous images of Luke—photographs of him accepting industry awards, speaking at conferences, and shaking hands over business deals. He looked devastating in all of them; obviously not someone who took a poor photograph.

"Honey?" Rebekah raised her glass and clinked it against Chloe's. "You'd better start looking for another job."

****

Monday arrived all too quickly for Chloe, having woken with a slightly fuzzy head on Sunday morning. After bidding her friend goodbye, she had taken herself and Jasper off for their weekly visit to her mother's, where the conversation had definitely not included anything about getting jiggy with her new boss.

Now sitting at her desk and taking a sip of steaming black coffee, she looked up to see Scott Howard leaning against the door jamb with a woeful expression. In his mid-thirties, with fair hair and an easy-going manner, Scott had joined the company three years ago as head of design, and they had always got on well together.

"So, you're abandoning me then?" He gave her an accusing look.

"I'm hardly abandoning you, Scott." She smiled at him over the top of her mug.

"But you know what I'm like." He pulled a face. "You know how forgetful I am when I'm in the middle of a design; you remind me what meetings I'm late for…you keep me out of trouble."

"Yes, I do, and I've spent an hour this morning

with Clare, who is going to be your new assistant." She couldn't help but smile at the truth in his words. "I've given her your schedule, told her about keeping on top of your appointments, and to make sure that she sets up alerts for herself to remind you half an hour before all your meetings."

"Really?" He brightened up a little.

"Yes, and I've even instructed her to look interested when you try and bore her senseless with endless pictures of your children."

Scott grinned unrepentantly. "What can I say? They're gorgeous kids."

"Yes, they are. Clearly, they take after their mother." She returned his smile.

He sobered a little and favoured her with a keen look. "Joking aside, how do you feel about your new role? Things going okay with Niall?"

She hesitated before responding. "It's still new, I guess. He's very different from John...and you, for that matter. And...well, I've not spent any time with Mr. Warwick yet, so who knows?"

"You'll do all right with Luke," he said with confidence. "I know this buyout has caused people to feel unsettled, but I see it as a positive thing. He's going to take this company forward, and I'm happy to be a part of it. He'll sort the wheat from the chaff."

She nodded and forced herself to smile when he straightened up.

"Anyway, I just wanted to say that I'll miss you, kid."

"I'm still here. I'm not going anywhere."

She stared into the empty doorway after he left, and wondered about that last remark. The conversation with Rebekah at the weekend had given her food for thought. She had not taken it seriously at the time—they had both been more than a little merry at that point—but since then she had found herself thinking that perhaps a new job might not be such a bad idea after all. Handing over the duties she had previously performed for Scott to Clare, one of the junior secretaries, had been an interesting task this morning. It was certainly an opportunity for Clare to prover herself capable of progressing further within the company, but it also served as a reminder to Chloe that she had worked at Hardaker's for five years. And although she enjoyed her job, she now wondered if she was simply coasting through life.

She felt safe here. When she had served the injunction on Chris last year, John Cameron had insisted all her telephone calls were to be screened, and made staff aware of the situation. Initially mortified by everyone knowing her business, it had proved the right thing to do when Chris had attempted to gain entry to the building. His attempt had been thwarted by two burly engineers and, to her knowledge, he had made one more unsuccessful attempt before apparently giving up and leaving her alone.

Did he know where she lived? She wasn't sure. He lived in Scarborough, half an hour's drive from Whitby, so it wasn't as if she ran the ongoing risk of bumping into him in town. But she had been paranoid about the possibility of him waiting for her outside work and following her home. So paranoid, in fact, that for the first few months she had driven a long and circuitous route home to her little cottage, taking over an hour to get home instead of the usual twenty minutes. More recently, though, she had relaxed and simply driven home, all thoughts of Chris gone.

A long discussion with Rebekah at the weekend had filled her with renewed determination to continue moving on, to refuse to allow him to frighten her anymore. They had agreed she would not apply for a renewal to the injunction, despite his unwelcome appearance the week before. Whatever Chris did or didn't do—and she had no real reason to believe he was going to cause her any trouble—Chloe decided she could handle it.

Similarly, she knew she couldn't stay at Hardaker's forever, simply because she felt safe there. She was a good PA, quick-thinking and efficient, but recently her role had lacked challenge. And with the added stress of now having to work so closely with Luke, perhaps it was time to move on. In fact, the more she thought about it, the more she grew to like the idea, and decided to register with an online recruitment agency when she got home that evening.

Chewing the end of her pencil, deep in concentration as she worked on the figures in front of her, she didn't look up immediately upon hearing the knock on the open office door. As a result, she was unprepared for her stomach performing a disconcerting somersault when Luke strode in, looking handsome in an expensive, perfectly tailored, charcoal grey suit. Despite the frantic thudding of her heart, she managed a calm, impersonal smile when he came to a stop in front of her desk.

"Morning, Chloe. How are you?"

"I'm good, thanks."

"I'm sorry I wasn't around much last week. Has

everything been okay?"

She blinked a little in surprise. "Yes, everything's fine. Um…if it's Niall you're looking for, I'm afraid he's not in yet."

"Oh, right. He forwarded a number of reports last week, but one of them seems to be an old version. Would you be able to let me have the most recent copy?"

"Of course. Which report do you need?"

Checking through her files, she realised the report he wanted related to one of several clients whom Niall insisted on dealing with personally, and which included keeping all electronic files on his personal drive, to which only he had access. Any paper copies would be locked in a filing cabinet in his office.

"Do you have the keys to his filing cabinet?" Luke frowned.

"Of course."

He followed her through to Niall's office as she went to the filing cabinet behind the desk, uncomfortably aware of his presence so close beside her. She quickly found the file he wanted and handed it to him.

"Thanks, I'll bring it back when I've finished." He paused, his lips pursed thoughtfully. "Does Niall have many clients he deals with personally?"

"Um…a few, I guess. As you saw, I have a list of the files so it's not as if he's secretive about it. He says they prefer the personal touch; makes them feel important, that kind of thing."

Luke appeared as if he was about to say something further, but in the end he simply nodded and left.

Catching herself staring after him, Chloe shoved at

the filing cabinet drawer, frowning when it refused to fully close. When it still wouldn't shut despite several attempts, she gave a frustrated sigh and pulled it open again as far as it would go, then reached in to see if she could find whatever was causing the obstruction. Her fingertips brushed the edge of something right at the very back, but she couldn't quite reach in far enough to grasp it. Looking around the office thoughtfully to see if there was anything she could use to dislodge it, her gaze fell on a ruler lying neatly to the side of Niall's desk. Armed with her new tool, she reached into the cabinet to jab at whatever was blocking the drawer. It worked. She heard something fall to the very bottom of the cabinet and, with a satisfied smile, closed the offending drawer before opening the bottom one and reaching into the back to lift whatever it was out.

It was a document folder, much like every other folder in the cabinet, except this one was unmarked, whereas all the others were clearly named for easy reference. Frowning slightly, she opened the folder and drew out the contents.

Her breath caught in her throat, and she blinked in shock.

The folder contained numerous digital color prints of the same man and woman. Some showed the couple sitting in a restaurant or walking across the street, while others were more intimate, and two fairly explicit.

Chloe stared at the contents of the folder, blinking rapidly as she tried to comprehend what she was looking at.

Why were they here in this folder, hidden at the back of Niall's cabinet? Did he know about them? She shook her head immediately. Idiot, of course he knew about them. Why else would they be in his office?

She cast a swift, fearful glance over her shoulder. If Niall found her in here with the folder, he would…Well, she didn't like to think what he would do. She shuffled quickly through the prints, swallowing against a sudden feeling of nausea. She was left in no doubt that the man was John Cameron, her former boss. But the young woman in the photographs was definitely not his wife, whom Chloe knew well. Several letters were tucked behind the photographs, and she pulled out the sheets of paper to read them, relieved not to have to look at the photographs a moment longer. Her relief was short-lived. The letters were from Niall Jefferson, clearly blackmailing her boss into early retirement.

Hardly able to believe what she was reading, she raised a shaking hand to her brow, thoughts whirling around her head. How had Niall got hold of these photographs? How could John do that to his wife?

More importantly, what was she going to do about it?

Her hands were shaking so hard that she risked dropping the folder and, closing her eyes, she forced herself to take a deep, steadying breath.

Come on, Chloe, think! Niall would be returning soon.

That last thought galvanised her into action, and she hurried through to her office to photocopy the entire contents of the folder before returning the original file to the back of the filing cabinet and locking it once more.

Trying to work quickly, terrified that Niall would come back and see what she was doing, she placed the photocopies—face down so that she didn't have to look at them—inside an envelope, and sealed it with shaking fingers. She gazed around the office, looking for somewhere to hide it; somewhere where no-one else could stumble across it as she had done. In the end, she taped it to the underside of her desk drawer, and locked it shut until she had calmed down and had chance to think clearly about what to do.

Glancing across at the wall clock, relief washed over her when she saw it was lunchtime. She snatched up her handbag, and fled the office, desperate to avoid Niall until she had regained some sort of composure.

****

Returning to the office an hour later, having walked aimlessly around Whitby's narrow, cobbled streets, Chloe hesitated in the doorway when she saw Niall's door was now closed. Her heart thumped in her chest at the thought of what he had done, of what was hidden in his filing cabinet, and she bit her lip, resisting the urge to turn and run. She forced herself to walk to the desk and take her seat, leaning forward to log into her laptop. She was staring at her screen as it flickered into life, when Luke strode through the door, and she jumped in surprise. He paused at her desk, was about to speak when his gaze swept her face, and a frown creased his forehead.

"Are you okay?"

The familiar gravelly voice and his obvious concern threatened her composure.

Tell him. Tell him what Niall has done.

But she couldn't. She couldn't shame John like that, and so she simply nodded her head, not trusting herself to speak.

He gave her a searching glance, clearly

unconvinced. But as the silence stretched between them, he eventually nodded. "Is Niall in?"

When she nodded again, he stared at her a moment longer before turning and going through to Niall's office. He left several minutes later with a curt 'thank you', walking straight past her and out into the corridor.

Within seconds, Niall appeared in the open doorway.

"In my office. Now." His words were clipped, and he returned to his desk without looking to see if she followed.

This was the moment she had been dreading. Taking a deep breath and striving for normality, Chloe walked through his door, trying desperately to mask her revulsion for the man.

He was pacing back and forth in front of his desk, his movements jerky, his fingers opening and closing into fists by his side.

"I remember a conversation we had recently, Chloe." His voice was quiet and even, although he continued to pace the floor. "Do you remember that conversation? The one about loyalty, and watching each other's backs? Do you remember that?" His voice rose, and he bit off the last word as if catching his temper.

"Yes, I do." She eyed him warily. Clearly close to losing his temper in a big way, he suddenly reminded her of Chris.

He nodded several times, his gaze on the floor while he continued to pace.

"Yes, I do," he mimicked. "And yet, this last week or so, our new MD has been all over my files like a bloody rash." His words were now peppered with obscenities, and instinctively Chloe took a step backwards towards the door. "Sniffing around all the departments, checking up on my figures, on my reporting, my spreadsheets. Asking questions, querying my calculations, my projections, my Every. Damned. Thing."

He suddenly stopped pacing and turned to stare at her. He was physically shaking with anger, his face an alarming shade of puce, and his fists were now curled into tight fists by his side. "Who the hell does he think he is? How dare he treat me like some bloody office junior?"

She strove to keep her breathing even, all thoughts of the hidden folder now forgotten as she stood immobile, hardly daring to move in case it triggered a reaction from him.

"And then I remembered. I remembered seeing the two of you, all cosy-cosy in the corridor…whispering." His face twisted at the memory. "You conniving little bitch!"

She gasped in shock, her mouth dropping open as he continued.

"You've been snooping around my files, haven't you? Passing information across to Warwick. Here, Mr. Warwick, why don't you look at this, Mr. Warwick? I'm a bit worried about these figures, Mr. Warwick. I don't think Niall knows what he's doing, Mr. Warwick," he sneered.

Tears of anger and humiliation flooded her eyes, but she blinked them away, determined not to be cowed by this hateful man. She suddenly knew without a doubt that Niall had something to hide. With a flash of clarity, she understood why he had been blackmailing John Cameron; her old boss must have found out about whatever Niall was up to.

"I haven't said anything to Luke." She lifted her chin with a confidence she didn't feel when he gave a disbelieving snort. "It hadn't even crossed my mind that there was anything wrong with the figures, that you were doing something wrong. But you are, aren't you? You're fixing the figures or something, and Luke has found out, just like John did."

Niall suddenly became very still, and his face— once puce—now drained of colour and his eyes narrowed dangerously. Chloe's knees began to tremble. Idiot. Why couldn't she keep her mouth shut?

"What did you say?" His voice was suddenly very calm and quiet.

Tempted to backtrack, instead she heard herself pressing on with what she knew. "You were blackmailing John Cameron. He found out what you were up to, and he left because you were blackmailing him. You disgust me."

His eyes widened and he began to laugh. "I disgust *you*?" He walked towards her slowly, still laughing, and she forced herself to stand firm. "I disgust you?"

Without warning, he lashed out with a backhander, cuffing her across the side of her head and sending her sprawling.

Chapter Five

Stunned and disorientated, Chloe scrambled to her feet, blinking away the stars filling her vision as she turned to face him where he stood calmly. She shook her head to rid herself of the ringing in her ears, and started to back away unsteadily, but Niall lunged forward, his hand closing around her neck like a vice. He shoved her hard against the wall, lifting her off her feet.

"You stupid, snooping little bitch. You think you're so clever?" Spittle flew from his lips as he spat the words out, his enraged face only inches from hers. "What were you hoping for? A promotion? A place in his bed? Or maybe this is what you wanted? This is what you like? You certainly had Cameron fooled, fawning all over you last year, telling us all how worried he was. *We need to look after Chloe. Oh, poor little Chloe, such an abusive ex-boyfriend.*"

He ignored her desperate gasps for breath. She was clawing at his hands as he continued to squeeze her throat. "What a load of crap! It's all you're good for. Women like you deserve everything you get. You've been begging for it."

His voice suddenly dropped to a whisper and he leaned even closer. She shrank from his hot, sour breath. "Would you like to know what I'm going to do to you?"

Fighting against the heaviness in her limbs, Chloe summoned up the strength to try and resist, kicking out at him, but her efforts were futile. His grip simply tightened, and darkness crept in around the edge of her vision as she began to lose consciousness.

The thunderous roar of blood in her ears drowned out the words he was shouting, but the next moment she fell to the floor when he released her without warning. Blinking away the tears streaming from her eyes, she drew in huge, painful gasps of air, her head confused and disoriented. A hand gently encircled her wrist and she cringed away with a cry of fear.

"Hey, hey, it's okay. It's me, it's Scott."

"Scott?" She shook her head to clear her vision, wincing when pain flared across her neck.

"Can you get to your feet if I help you?"

She managed a slight nod, and let him help her to her feet, allowing him to put his arm around her shoulders as she attempted to steady herself. Her eyes widened when she saw Luke restraining Niall, holding his left arm high up behind his back, and forcing his head down on the desk. Jeff was hovering in the middle of the room, clearly torn between helping Chloe and assisting Luke.

"Scott, can you make sure Chloe is all right? Get her to the hospital if necessary. Jeff, I think you'd better call the police." Quiet and calm, the clipped words betrayed his anger as Luke turned his attention back to Niall, still face down on the desk. "You bastard. I underestimated you. Had you down as someone who contented himself with defrauding the company out of thousands of pounds. More fool me. You're even more pathetic than I imagined. Is that how you get your kicks? Assaulting a woman?"

Despite being pinned against the desk, Niall grinned. "Don't pretend you're any different, Warwick. Don't pretend you wouldn't love to get that pretty little neck in your hands."

Scott swiftly ushered Chloe into her own office, effectively masking Luke's response to Niall. But as he closed the door behind him, she could hear the soft murmur of voices, sounding absurdly as if they were engaged in a perfectly normal conversation.

****

Fifteen minutes later, Luke stepped through into the outer office—leaving Jeff watching over Niall—and quietly closed the door behind him. Expecting the office to be empty, he stopped in surprise, his gaze narrowing when he saw Scott and Chloe standing in the middle of the room, Scott's hands on her shoulders.

He was thrown by the acute stab of jealousy that ripped through him as he observed the obvious concern in the other man's body language, the closeness of their stance. He swallowed hard before allowing himself to speak.

"Is everything all right? I wasn't expecting you to be here, Chloe."

"I'm trying to persuade her to speak to her doctor." Scott made no effort to move away. "She's trying to carry on as if nothing happened."

"I see," said Luke quietly, after a slight pause. "Scott, the police are down in reception. Would you mind giving us five minutes, and then bringing them up to Niall's office?"

Scott nodded immediately and turned back to

Chloe.

"If you need anything, kiddo, just ask."

He gave her shoulder one last squeeze before walking across to Luke and shaking his hand.

"No idea what the hell happened in there, but that was nicely done." He grinned. "Good to have you on the team."

Luke waited until Scott had left, and then shut the door behind him before turning back to Chloe. She started moving round the office, picking up papers and pulling open the filing cabinet to put them away. Papers tidied up, she moved across to her own desk, tapped on the keyboard, clicked the mouse, and then hurried across to the printer where she waited impatiently as it began spitting out sheets of paper. All this was completed while studiously ignoring him.

"Chloe, what are you doing?" He strove to keep his voice quiet and calm.

"What do you think I'm doing?" She gave him a brief, slightly irritable smile. "Printing off the papers for your meeting this afternoon."

He blew out a long, slow breath. "I've cancelled my meetings for this afternoon."

"Oh. Well, it would have been nice if you had told me."

She had not met his eyes once since he had left Niall's office, and he gazed at her in frustration, not knowing quite what to do, but acutely aware of the slight tremor in her hands and the pallor of her skin.

"I think you should see a doctor—"

"No." She bit her lip and took a breath. "I'm perfectly fine, and I don't need to see a doctor. I'm assuming you'll be re-arranging the meeting, so I'll keep these papers ready for when you need them."

Shuffling the papers, she clipped them together before sliding them into a new document wallet and writing on the outside in neat capital letters.

"Chloe, will you stop?" It was Luke's turn to catch himself and take a calming breath. "If you won't see a doctor, then at least go home and get some rest. The police will want a statement from you, but I'm sure you can do that later in the week."

She stared at him. "No. I'm not making a statement. I'm not pressing charges. I just want to forget it."

"What do you mean, you're not pressing charges?"

"I think it's an easy enough concept." She held his gaze defiantly before giving a weary sigh, her shoulders sagging. "I'm not pressing charges. There's little point. I know what Niall's like, he'll...he'll twist everything. If he's been defrauding the company then it's all over, he'll be gone. That's all I want."

"But that's ridiculous, you can't just forget it."

"Yes, I can, actually." She straightened her shoulders. "It's absolutely none of your business, and you can't make me do anything. I will not press charges against Niall."

An uneasy feeling settled in the pit of Luke's stomach. There was something else going on here, and whatever it was, it wasn't good. Silence stretched across the increasing distance between them, and he moved towards the window, staring absently out over the harbour. Eventually, he turned back to Chloe.

"What happened in there?" He shook his head, gesturing his confusion. "Why did he attack you?"

She shrugged, dropping her gaze and starting to reorder the folders on her desk.

"It wasn't about the fraud," he persisted. "You didn't know about that. So, what was it?"

Carefully stacking the folders one on top of the other, she made sure they were lined up with the edge of the desk before turning towards him, her gaze deliberately focussed two feet to the left of him.

"It was personal."

Luke felt his jaw drop. He hadn't been expecting that.

"Personal?" He stared at her, thrown off-guard. What the Hell did she mean by *personal*?

Again, she shrugged, but this time she remained silent.

"Chloe—" He started to move towards her, but froze when her head snapped up and she backed away behind her desk. Again, that squirming, nauseous feeling in his stomach as he recognised what she had done. *Did she think he was going to hurt her? My God, is that what she thought?*

Luke swallowed hard, unable to take his eyes from her face, and saw her give an apologetic smile, obviously recognising his shock at her retreat.

All he wanted to do was to fold her in his arms, tell her everything would be all right. Instead, he leant against Mary's vacant desk, legs crossed at the ankles, and arms folded across his chest.

"You should go home," he said quietly.

"No, I don't need to go home. I'm perfectly capable—"

"No, you are not." He cut her off sharply, closing his eyes briefly as he struggled to hide his irritation. "Will you do as you are told for once? I've never known anyone so damned wilful."

He shook his head before carrying on in a softer tone. "Look, you've just been assaulted, you're badly shaken up and, as your boss, I am telling you to go home. Take tomorrow off as well if you need to. But, if not, I'll see you in the morning. Okay?"

Sudden tears shimmered in her eyes and she quickly bent down to reach under her desk, clearly trying to hide her distress. Having retrieved her handbag, Chloe slipped it over her shoulder and walked around the desk.

"Fine. I'll see you tomorrow."

"Only if you feel up to it. I'll text you later to check you're okay."

"No. Please don't. I'll be perfectly fine." She briefly met his gaze. "I'll see you tomorrow."

****

Chloe walked out into the car park and stood for a moment, fighting against a sudden urge to cry. Tilting her head back, she drew in a long, deep breath, her eyes lifting above the rows of houses, huddled together as they clung tightly onto the steep walls of the cliffs, up to the cloudless blue sky above. She knew where she wanted to go, and it wasn't home. Instead of turning towards her car, she walked out onto Church Street, her steps slow at first, but gathering pace as the need for escape built within her chest. The street narrowed as it reached the more popular heart of the old town, crowded with tourists meandering without purpose.

She bit back a sob of frustration as she twisted and turned through the crowds, murmuring 'excuse me' and 'sorry' as she blindly pressed on past the Blitz Café and the Whitby Jet Shop, until she rounded the corner to reach the famous one hundred and ninety-nine steps.

Desperate now, she sprinted up the steps, breathing hard, but determined not to stop. She flew through the crowds of more sensible tourists who were taking a more leisurely ascent and pausing to rest on the benches at the edge of the steps, some of them taking the opportunity to snap a photograph of the stunning views of the town below.

Reaching the top and wincing at the pain in her throat as she drew in huge, gasping breaths, Chloe began to half run, half walk past the Church of St. Mary. For once she was unmoved by the uneven rows of gravestones gathered around the church, the names of their occupants lost forever as the sandstone succumbed to the elements, the heartfelt last words about loved ones replaced by the pockmarks caused by a bitter sea wind.

Barely aware of the strange glances being cast towards her—running as she was in her smart work clothes and heeled shoes as if being pursued—she ignored the queries of concern from people as she tore past them. Reaching the walled garden of the old Abbey House, once home to the Cholmley family, but now a souvenir shop and entrance to the Abbey itself, she slowed to a walk. She drew up outside the main doors, and made an effort to collect herself before walking in, forcing a smile at the young girl on the ticket desk. A regular visitor and fully paid-up member of English Heritage, Chloe was waved through with a smile, and she ran lightly up the stairs before walking quickly along the length of the exhibition room above.

At last, she walked out into the bright sunlight, emotion threatening to overwhelm her as she stared across the headland to where the ruins of Whitby Abbey rose up before her, calm and serene. Her vision blurred as tears filled her eyes and she blinked them away, swallowing hard against the lump in her throat.

She walked slowly along the path towards the Abbey, allowing the familiar ruins to calm her, drawing on the serenity that pervaded the site regardless of the many tourists milling around. She loved this place. Despite its skeletal, ruined structure, the Abbey had an aura of strength, of calm and peacefulness; a feeling of being able to withstand anything. On days like today, with little wind and the warmth of the sun beating down, Chloe could imagine the Benedictine monks feeling as if they had found a little part of heaven on earth. And yet, here on the edge of the cliffs, the Abbey was exposed to the brutal elements of the weather and everything nature could throw at it. Life would have been hard here. But the Abbey had endured.

She walked on through the nave and out the other side, making her way to the perimeter wall running parallel with the cliff edge. She leaned against the wall, staring down at the harbour below, before lifting her gaze to cliffs at the opposite side, searching for one little white dot in particular. There it was, almost too far away to see as the headland curved away out of sight. One little white blob. Her cottage. Her sanctuary.

Calmer now, she walked across to a solitary bench and took a seat. Only then did she allow herself to reflect on what had happened in the office this afternoon.

Had it been real?

She gingerly fingered her throat, wincing slightly at the tender spot on each side. Not some nightmare then.

Niall had attacked her. Not only that, but it had been ominously similar to the way Chris had attacked her the night she left him, knocking her to the floor and pinning her up against the wall. What was it about her that made men think it was all right to do that?

Because it was your fault.

She closed her eyes, shaking her head as a small moan escaped her lips. No! It wasn't her fault…was it?

You pushed him. You knew Niall was angry and yet you carried on pushing, telling him he disgusted you. What did you expect? You deserved it.

Chloe shot to her feet restlessly, looking around her as if to escape her own thoughts. Luke. She wanted Luke; wanted to hear him tell her everything was all right, that it wasn't her fault. She longed for his strength, his calmness, his kindness.

How do you know he wouldn't do the same, given the chance?

That voice inside her head made her pause. Her mother would tell her he was no different to the rest. That there was something about Chloe that brought out the worst in men. Maybe even Luke.

She shook her head. No. Not Luke. She wouldn't believe that. Her head told her that none of this was her fault, but her heart remained convinced otherwise. That same heart, though, was certain Luke would never lift a finger against her, or any other woman.

Sinking down onto the seat once more, she closed her eyes and concentrated on taking long, slow deep breaths. "I am a good person. I am not worthless." She whispered the mantra over and over to herself until she felt calm once more.

Maybe one day she would even believe it.

Lifting her handbag onto her knee, she took out her phone, shading the screen with her hand. No messages, no texts, no missed calls. What had she expected? Now that he was her boss, Luke had her mobile number so he could contact her if needed, but she had just told him not to text her. So, why was she disappointed when he had taken her at her word?

Angry with the little voice in her head, the one that wouldn't shut up, she pushed herself up from the seat and started to walk briskly back to the Abbey House. But still that nagging voice whispered that perhaps he might text her later.

After all, he would if he really cared, wouldn't he?

Chapter Six

Luke stood by his office window, staring down into the car park, hands shoved in his pockets. He was used to having to sort out problems, unravelling failing business accounts, identifying where a business was going wrong. It was what the Warwick Company Ltd did. But this was something different. In a matter of weeks, his life had been turned upside down.

His gaze was drawn to a car entering the car park, and he watched as Chloe's little black car pulled into a vacant space. He frowned. Right there was the main reason for his current unsettled state of mind. His usual cool-headed reasoning had flown through the window the moment he had seen her down on that beach. He had so very nearly sent her a text last night, desperate to reassure himself that she was all right, but she had been so adamant about not contacting her. He'd written, re-written, and deleted at least five texts, abiding by the rules he had set himself long ago; the first being never to mix business with pleasure. Sticking to that rule had finally persuaded him to toss his phone in a drawer where it couldn't tempt him.

Never mix business with pleasure.

He gave a weary sigh; Chloe was seriously testing his resolve on that one.

Despite himself, he couldn't help but smile as she got out of the car. Her quirkiness always made him smile. She dressed smartly for work but still managed to retain that kooky edge, with a long, black, fishtail skirt, black Victorian-style kitten heeled boots, and usually a high-necked, white blouse. Perfectly smart, perfectly unusual. And totally unaware of how very sexy she looked sashaying along the corridors.

Halfway across the car park, she stopped and looked sharply to her left. Luke moved a little closer to the window, wondering what had caught her eye. Unable to see anything unusual, his gaze strayed back to Chloe who was now walking slowly over to where the industrial recycling bins stood in the corner. After a moment, she crouched down and held out her hand, clearly trying to coax something out from behind one of the bins. He watched in fascination when she called out to one of the engineers as he came out of the warehouse. Luke frowned. He'd met the engineer briefly last week. What was his name? John? Mike? That was it—Mike.

Mike wandered over to join her and he, too, crouched down as she pointed towards whatever it was she was coaxing out.

After a few moments of animated conversation, peppered with a lot of shaking his head and scratching his chin, Mike was obviously persuaded to undertake an errand, and he walked off towards the cabin that served as a staffroom for the workmen. He returned a few moments later with a mug and a saucer, which he handed to Chloe.

Entranced by this little scene, Luke folded his arms and waited to see what would happen next.

Chloe crouched down once more, placing the saucer on the floor near to the bin, and poured what Luke imagined was milk into the saucer. She held out her hand, rubbing her fingers together and he could imagine her making soft crooning noises to whatever it was hiding behind the recycling bins. He was curious to see if it would be brave enough to come out.

Hunger eventually overcame its fear of strangers because, after a few minutes, a small, bedraggled cat inched towards the saucer and began warily lapping at the milk. Chloe shooed Mike away and, after a moment, slowly reached out to stroke the pathetic little animal. It carried on drinking, as if it hadn't eaten in days. In no time at all, the milk was gone, and it was looking up at her, its mouth opening as it mewled for more. Without any obvious concern for her jacket, Chloe scooped up the cat and held it close, stroking its fur.

As she turned to speak to Mike, who was still obediently keeping his distance, Luke saw the distress on her face, and he shook his head. She cared so much about everything. Even Mike appeared moved by her concern, because he lifted a hand as if to stop her in mid-conversation, reaching into his pocket and drawing out his mobile phone. Hanging up a few minutes later, he looked very pleased with himself and nodded towards Chloe. All three of them waited: Mike and Chloe in the car park, and Luke up in his office, unobserved.

They didn't have long to wait. Five minutes later, another car drew into the car park and pulled up beside them. A woman got out and, reaching into the back seat, lifted out a cat basket. Luke frowned. Was she from the veterinary practice? She'd got here pretty quickly, if so. The woman carefully took the cat from Chloe and placed it in the basket, nodding reassuringly to her as she did so. Luke watched the interaction between the three of them, coming to the conclusion that the woman was probably Mike's wife, which would explain the speed with which she had arrived. He seemed to remember Mike lived within walking distance of the boatyard.

Within a few minutes, the woman had left with the cat, presumably on her way to the vets; Mike had returned to the warehouse; and Chloe was left standing in the car park, somewhat belatedly looking down to see if the cat had muddied her jacket. Laughing softly to himself, Luke returned to his desk and waited for her to make her way up to the office.

****

Chloe was still absently brushing at her jacket when she walked in, and immediately saw Luke sitting behind Niall's desk through the open door. He looked up as she shrugged off the jacket, and beckoned for her to come in as he walked across to the filter coffee machine on a small table in the office. He poured her a black coffee without asking for her preference, and placed it on the desk in front of her as she sat down. He looked at her searchingly for a moment, and she saw his gaze drop to her throat, his lips tightening when he saw the bruises she had tried to conceal.

He looked as if he wanted to say something, but obviously thought better of it and instead returned to his seat on the other side of the desk. "Are you all right?"

She nodded, lifting her chin, but unwilling to trust herself to speak after hearing the concern in his voice. She swallowed hard and licked her lips to buy herself a second or two before speaking. "Another rescue. It's getting to be a habit. I'm sorry."

She saw him frown, and carried on before he could answer. "I don't want to be a damsel in distress, relying on some bloody man to rescue me all the time." She winced and smiled apologetically. "No offence."

"None taken." He smiled. "And I don't see you as a damsel in distress; not at all."

She couldn't help it. "What do you see?"

"A woman who is stronger than she realises. Someone who is sometimes in the wrong place at the wrong time. Someone who cares deeply about others; four-legged friends in particular."

She looked up quickly at the laughter in his voice.

"What happened to the cat?"

She stared at him in surprise, her mind working quickly, and then her gaze travelled to the window behind him, and which overlooked the carpark.

She gave a soft laugh. "Poor little thing, it was half starved. I could feel its ribs when I picked it up. Mike phoned his wife and she agreed to take it to the vet. It was really kind of her."

"It was indeed."

There was a long pause before she dared to ask the question. "So…um, so what happened with Niall after I left yesterday?"

Luke sobered immediately and leaned back in his chair. "Well, the Board has some tough decisions to make. We either take Niall down the legal route for fraud, or we let him go quietly without too much of a fuss."

She gaped at him. "Why on earth would we do that?"

He shrugged. "To save the company's reputation? Taking Niall to court would be lengthy, costly, and very public."

"But...but we can't just let him get away with it."

"It happens more frequently than you would think. Reputation is everything in business. To have your dirty laundry aired in public, to admit to being unaware of fraud on this scale, over such a long period of time, is not something to be proud of."

"But, what he did..." She couldn't continue, could feel herself choking up.

"I'm not saying we're not going to take him to court. I'm saying the Board has to weigh up their options. Look, I don't want you to worry over this." He paused, looking at her thoughtfully. "Have you had any more thoughts about making a statement?"

She shook her head, dropping her gaze to her hands knotted in her lap. "I haven't changed my mind."

His only response was a slight shake of the head, and he reached forward to take a swallow of his coffee, gesturing to her as yet untouched cup.

"Okay. Well, in terms of getting back to business, it would appear we have quite a bit of recruitment to undertake. I've arranged for a couple of people from the Warwick Company Ltd to stand in for some of the posts, John Cameron's in particular. But in terms of Niall's job, I'll be standing in for him for the time being. I'm afraid I'll probably have to rely on you for a while."

Luke paused briefly to collect his thoughts before carrying on.

"I know there has been some speculation as to what role Jeff will take in the company following the transfer of ownership. He's been very honest with me, and admitted that this last year has really taken its toll. Niall's betrayal and his ability to do that right under Jeff's nose has knocked him for six." He paused for a moment. "He's going to retire at the end of the month, but I've asked him to stay on as a non-executive member of the board. His expertise will be invaluable."

She nodded slowly. Jeff had visibly aged in the few weeks, looking as if he had all the cares of the world on his shoulders. Having lost John Cameron so suddenly, learning of the fraud must have been another huge blow.

"As I said, I have someone coming in to replace John next week and he will be bringing his current assistant with him," Luke carried on before she could speak. "My own assistant, Elise, will be joining me in a little over a month's time."

Chloe stared at him wordlessly, not sure if she had understood him correctly; was he saying that she was out of a job?

"This company is in deep trouble and currently running at a loss, as I'm sure you are aware, mainly due to Niall's creativity with the budgets. However, I remain convinced that this is a viable organisation. I wouldn't have taken it over otherwise, and I intend to stay on as managing director for the foreseeable future. So, until Elise is able to join me, I will need you to work alongside me as my assistant. I need someone who knows the company and whom I can trust to work quickly and effectively."

He paused, waiting for her response.

"Right, and are you saying that, in a little over a month's time, when your assistant arrives, I will be out of a job? Just like that?" She stared at him in disbelief, unsure whether to laugh or cry.

Luke looked taken aback. "No, no, of course not."

He came around the desk and sat on the edge, frowning at her. "We are still a finance director short, and obviously we'll be replacing him. He will need an assistant, but I also want to take a little time to get a true picture of the company and what the strategic team needs to look like. If I'm being honest, I think your skills have been wasted to date. I want to consider if there is a way for us to create a new role that utilises your skills more effectively; if that's something you are interested in, of course."

****

Chloe returned to her desk, sinking gratefully into her seat, and dropping her head into her hands. What was it she had been thinking last week? *I wonder what surprises the next week will bring.* Well, she'd had enough surprises now. She wanted everything to stop, to go back to normal.

The shrill peal of the telephone interrupted her thoughts, and she lifted her head to stare at the offending instrument for a few moments before answering it.

"Chloe, is that you? It's John, John Cameron. How are you?"

It took her a few seconds to register who it was; she had not heard from John since he'd left. She had a sudden vision of those awful photographs and closed her eyes, forcing herself to respond to his query about her health.

"I'm fine, thank you." She swallowed and forced herself to smile. "How are you?"

"Good, good. I'm well, thank you." John's voice sounded reassuringly familiar, and she felt herself relaxing. She had always got on so well with him, had looked up to him and admired him. "I know you're probably wondering why I'm ringing you out of the blue. Well, I wanted to run something by you, and wondered if you would allow me to buy you lunch one day this week?"

She hesitated. If she refused, John would be hurt, and would know something was wrong. Glancing down at her desk drawer, she thought of the envelope still taped underneath, and was unable to prevent a shiver of revulsion at the contents.

"Chloe? Are you still there?"

"Yes sorry, John, someone walked into the office," she said, trying to buy herself some time. Whatever he had done, she couldn't just cut him off. "Um, yes, of course, lunch would be lovely. Shall we say tomorrow at one?"

May as well get it over with.

****

John Cameron looked happy and relaxed in a pair of cream chinos and a pale blue polo shirt as he rose to meet her, his gunmetal grey hair immaculately groomed as usual. They had agreed to meet at a popular restaurant a little way out of town and, although fairly busy, John had chosen a table in a quiet area of the conservatory.

"Chloe, it's good to see you." He leaned across to kiss her cheek as she arrived.

"John." She smiled as he helped her with her seat, his old-fashioned manners as impeccable as ever, and was relieved to find that she was genuinely pleased to see him. "You look well."

"Thank you, my dear." He settled himself in the seat opposite, but his smile faded slightly when he observed her a little more closely. "I wish I could say the same about you. You look rather pale, if you don't mind me saying. Is everything all right?"

She hesitated, making a 'sort of' gesture with her hands, before elaborating when he raised his eyebrows. "To be honest, it's been an eventful few weeks since you left. Niall has been sacked...for fraud...and he, well, he attacked me."

Having initially looked almost satisfied, John sat forward abruptly. "He did what?"

"I'm sorry, I didn't mean to come out with that quite so bluntly. I had intended to sort of ease it into the conversation." She giggled a little, and then grimaced as the action aggravated her throat, still tender from the assault. "I'm fine, it was nothing, really. Luke came in at the right moment and dragged him off me."

John stared at her, his mouth working for a moment before he found his voice. "Chloe, I'm so sorry. I had no idea he would go to such lengths..."

"I don't think anyone did."

She paused as the waitress came to take their order before continuing. "But you knew about Niall, didn't you? About the fraud?"

She gave a slight smile when he simply nodded wordlessly. He cleared his throat as if to speak, but she forced herself to carry on. "John...I...I saw the letters from Niall...the photographs."

He stared at her, and the colour drained from his face to leave him ashen. He tried to speak, but no sound left his mouth, and he turned away but not before she had seen the haunted look in his eyes.

She wanted to weep for him. He was such a proud, straightforward man; whatever he had done, he didn't deserve to be humiliated, and she regretted bringing the subject up. She glanced across the conservatory. Fortunately, it was still relatively quiet, and no-one seemed to have noticed his distress.

"Oh John, please don't. Please don't be upset." She reached forward to touch his arm.

After a moment he straightened, and turned his gaze to meet hers. His eyes were unnaturally bright, and he dabbed at them with a napkin before clearing his throat and reaching for his glass to take a sip of water.

"I feel so ashamed." He lifted his chin and gave her a quick, tight smile. "They're not real, you know, the photographs. They're not true. I would never, never do anything to hurt Sarah."

Surprise and relief washed over Chloe. "They're not? Then what happened?"

"Control, leverage. Call it what you want." He looked away in disgust. "It was Mary who first became suspicious about some of Niall's financial accounting. An unusual amount of additional stock, too many casual workers, that kind of thing. She started to keep a separate spreadsheet of her own, highlighting the areas she wasn't sure were correct. It was difficult to be sure, with Niall dealing with some clients personally." John shook his head, his voice shaking slightly but getting stronger. "However, she began to see an increasing number of more significant anomalies, and so she came to me for advice. She didn't want to approach Jeff straight away in case she was wrong. My mistake was to give Niall the benefit of the doubt. I decided to speak to him, give him the chance to explain the discrepancies."

He paused as the waitress appeared with their food, and he leaned back in his chair, his face pale. He managed to thank the waitress, but made no attempt to eat.

"And his response to my questions?" He gave a hollow, bitter laugh. "He took out a folder from his cabinet and slid it across the table to me. Told me that it should allay any concerns I might have. I believe you've seen the contents of that folder."

"But that's awful." Chloe was horrified. "Only…why didn't you tell someone? Why did you let him blackmail you into retiring if the photographs were fake?"

John flexed his shoulders uncomfortably, pushing around the contents of his plate with his fork. "I couldn't put Sarah in that position. I know she wouldn't have doubted me, we trust each other implicitly, but you know the old saying, *no smoke without fire*. People would always talk, always wonder, assume the worst, and I didn't want Sarah to have to put up with that. So, I agreed to leave. It's not as if I had many years left anyway."

He looked across at her, and Chloe saw the uncertainty in his eyes, the desperate need for her to understand. She shook her head slowly, reaching across to clasp his hand. What Niall had done to this poor man, this good man, was dreadful. She believed his assertion that the photographs were fake, had no doubts whatsoever, but she couldn't help but wish he had been that little bit stronger. Just strong enough to call Niall's bluff.

No sooner had the thought entered her head than she was ashamed of herself. That was unfair. She couldn't even begin to understand how John had felt, and it was wrong to sit in judgement of his actions. He had done what he thought was best.

"Mary left also, as you know. I think Niall made some thinly veiled threats." John withdrew his hand, and curled his fingers into a fist on the table. "That is something I am truly ashamed about. I shouldn't have allowed him to intimidate Mary. And now I find that he assaulted you." He covered his eyes briefly with his hand as he struggled to contain his distress. "Had I known what he was truly capable of, I might have acted differently."

"You did what you thought was best at the time." The words sounded lame even to her own ears, but he didn't seem to notice. Now that he had started, he clearly needed to unburden himself.

"I agreed to retire on the understanding that Niall would destroy all copies and files containing the photographs," he continued. "Obviously, I realise now that I was far too trusting in all respects. But I want you to know that, despite my cowardice in allowing him to blackmail me and intimidate Mary, I did so with the knowledge that Luke Warwick was taking over the company. I had, and continue to have, the utmost respect and admiration for that man. I knew he would find out what Niall had been up to and take decisive action…particularly after I met with him and passed across a copy of Mary's spreadsheet."

Chloe gasped and looked up at him in surprise.

He gave a gentle, knowing smile. "I was a coward, my dear, but perhaps not so much as I could have been." The colour was gradually returning to his face. "I was unable to bring myself to explain the reason for my sudden retirement, to expose Sarah to that kind of speculation—and that remains true to this day. I feel truly humiliated to think that you had to see those photographs, even though they are fake, and that…that…person in them isn't me."

"Oh John, please don't think about it a moment longer." She leaned across the table to grasp his forearm once more. "You have no reason to be ashamed. I think you acted with honour and dignity, and you did take action; you passed the information about Niall on to Luke."

"But to think that he actually attacked you. I can't even begin—"

"I want you to stop." She ducked her head to meet his gaze. "It's over. I'm fine, you're fine, and Niall is gone. It's done and we need never talk about it again."

"You're right, of course." He took a deep breath and straightened his shoulders, picking up his cutlery and gesturing to their meal. "And perhaps we ought to try and do justice to this delicious food while I tell you what it is I wanted to discuss with you."

Chloe listened as John told her about his eldest son's newest venture. Mark was a talented landscape photographer, and had recently leased a prime retail unit in the heart of Whitby's old town, where he intended to showcase and sell his framed prints. He was now looking for someone to manage both the shop and the online sales, to enable him to concentrate on his photography.

She smiled and nodded, wondering if he had asked her to lunch just to share his son's achievements.

"You should pop down and see the shop, it's a fantastic space with a good deal of passing trade. Mark was extremely lucky to get such a prime location." Finishing his meal, John carefully put his knife and fork together on the empty plate. "There's a small area in the shop for an additional display, complete with its own window."

He waited expectantly. "It's perfect."

Chloe stared at him blankly. "Perfect for what?"

"Why, for your jewellery, of course," he said, giving a short laugh at her perplexed expression. "I'm obviously not explaining myself very well. I've spoken to Mark about you, about how organised, efficient, and business-like you are; how you would be perfect to run his shop. I also told him about you making your own jewellery and how you always wanted to make it into your own business."

It was her turn to be struck dumb, unable to think of anything to say.

"Mark immediately offered to let you have the small display area for your jewellery," said John, clearly pleased with himself. "It would give you a chance to dip your toe in the water, risk-free."

She could feel the excitement bubbling in her chest. "Are you…are you serious? Would Mark really allow me to do that?"

"Yes, absolutely. It was his idea, but I wasn't sure if I could persuade you to leave Hardaker's."

"He does know that I know absolutely nothing about photography?"

"You don't need to. My son is looking for someone to manage the shop and promote the business, both of which you have a good deal of experience in," he dismissed her concerns. "And, although he can't offer any increase, he can match your current salary."

Chloe covered her mouth with her hands to bite back her excitement. It sounded wonderful; almost too good to be true. And to be offered this opportunity now, just when she was thinking she needed something new?

"It sounds wonderful, but...I really need to give it some thought. Would Mark be able to give me the weekend to think about it?"

John agreed it was a reasonable request and, when they left the restaurant, gave her a fatherly embrace, before climbing into his car and leaving her staring thoughtfully after him and wondering if perhaps this was fate.

****

The rest of the week passed without event and, although they worked together closely, not by a flicker in those green eyes did Luke acknowledge the intimacy they had previously shared. It was an exquisite agony for Chloe; just being in the same room as him caused her heart to thud painfully in her chest, and she had great difficulty in concentrating whenever he was near or leant close to explain a certain point. What made it worse was that he seemed to have no such problems around her, and she occasionally wondered if the time she had spent curled up in his arms was nothing but a figment of her fevered imagination.

As the days passed by, it became increasingly obvious just how he had managed to build up a large and successful company by himself at such a young age. He had a brilliant business mind and, if she worked long hours, then he worked longer. He was always there before she arrived in the morning, and continued until late into the night—long after she had gone home—if the emails he sent were anything to go by.

Tidying her desk before she left on Friday night, she paused for a moment, chewing her lip thoughtfully. She had agreed to let John know her decision by this weekend, but was torn. Luke's discussion regarding a possible new role within the company had given her something else to think about. How typical that, having worked in the same role for a number of years, she had now been offered two new opportunities within a week. She was also really enjoying working with Luke, and wasn't sure if she was willing to give that up.

But why? Why did she love working with him? She forced herself to really consider what was happening and, after a moment shook her head slowly. It wasn't just that she loved working with Luke. The truth was much more frightening than that.

She was falling in love him. Not just working for him, but the man himself.

She sank into her chair, her knees suddenly giving way now she had finally admitted to herself what she was feeling. She had known from the first night they met that she was vulnerable to him, but it was obvious the feeling wasn't mutual. Covering her face with her hands, she rested her elbows on the desk and breathed through her disappointment. Luke's attitude to her this last week had been friendly and respectful, but distant. Besides which, he had spelled it out clearly enough when they were sitting in his kitchen; he was not looking for a relationship.

Her mother's voice rang in her ears: *I told you so, didn't I? When will you ever learn?*

Chloe straightened her shoulders, dropped her

hands from her face, and lifted her chin. It was clear what she needed to do. She would take up John's offer to work for his son, and extricate herself from Luke's life with her dignity intact. Well, extricate herself from his working life. After all, she still had access to the private beach they shared. She still had that...

Deliberately ignoring that last thought, she switched off her laptop and turned to knock on his office door. She popped her head around to say goodnight, pretending her stomach hadn't given a little flip when he beckoned her in.

"I'm leaving myself in a couple of minutes. I was wondering if you needed a lift to the party tonight."

She swallowed hard, thanking her lucky stars that he hadn't offered earlier in the week when she would have had no excuse or, more correctly, no motivation to politely refuse. The party tonight was both a welcome and a farewell party—welcome to the Warwick Company Ltd staff who would be joining the firm, and a farewell to Jeff Hardaker.

"No, thank you. I already have a lift."

His eyebrows lifted slightly, and for a moment his eyes glittered with an unreadable emotion. But after a slight pause, he simply nodded and gave a half smile. "Okay. I'll see you later then."

Chapter Seven

"Will you stop fidgeting?" Sean smiled, and offered Chloe his arm. "You look really pretty."

"Thank you, and I'm sorry, I can't help it. I'm really nervous, which is stupid, I know, considering it's only a work's do." She smiled apologetically as they walked into the hotel's function room. "And thank you for coming with me tonight. I know Rebekah persuaded you to, but I really appreciate it. I didn't want to come on my own."

"Hey, no problem. Happy to be your rent-a-guy any time." He grinned, taking her hand, and tucking it under his elbow. "Bek will be back from her swanky business trip tonight, and has given me strict instructions to get as much gossip as I can. Just so you know, there is a price to be paid. Right, let's see if there's anything to drink at this party."

Left alone while he made his way through to the crowded bar, Chloe smoothed her dress over her hips, breathing long and slow as she tried to ignore the butterflies in her stomach. The simple black floor-length silk dress usually made her feel confident, but not tonight. Scanning the crowd, her gaze sought out Luke, but couldn't find him. Not quite sure if that made her feel more or less nervous, she couldn't help but remember the last time she had been at a similar party…the one that had ended with her throwing herself at Luke, and him rejecting her kisses.

Nice one, Chloe. Great start to the evening, let's think about the worst thing that happened.

"Hey." Soft, gravelly, and familiar, Luke's voice in her ear made her jump. "You okay? You look a bit…troubled?"

She blushed and waved her hand dismissively. "Oh no, I'm fine. I was… thinking…about something."

She managed a bright smile and was relieved when the quizzical frown wrinkling Luke's brow cleared. "You look beautiful."

Her smile widened. She couldn't help it. When he said things like that, it made her heart race. "Thank you."

"The bar's not too bad at the moment, got served fairly easily." Sean appeared at her side, and handed her a glass. "

Feeling awkward all of a sudden, she tried to ignore the heat creeping along her throat. "Um…thank you." She swallowed and waved a hand towards Luke, keeping her gaze firmly fixed on Sean's amused brown eyes. "Um, Sean, this is my boss, Luke Warwick."

"Luke?" She forced herself to face him, but couldn't bring herself to lift her gaze any higher than his bow tie. It was hand-tied, she noticed. "This is…This is Sean."

There was a pause as both men clearly waited for her to perhaps elaborate a little, but when she remained silent, Sean reached forward to shake Luke's hand.

"Good to meet you." He grinned, and slipped a hand around Chloe's waist to pull her into his side. "And I understand we have you to thank for saving

Chloe's life that night down on the beach?"

Luke nodded slowly. "Something like that." His gaze swept from one to the other.

An awkward little pause followed, which was fortunately broken by the arrival of Jeff Hardaker. "Luke, Chloe, I'm so sorry for interrupting," he gave an apologetic smile to Chloe before turning to Luke. "Would you mind dreadfully if I borrowed you for a moment?"

"Of course." He nodded immediately. "If you'll excuse me?" His voice was cool and distant, his smile brief, before turning away and following Jeff across the room.

"So that's Luke Warwick," said Sean thoughtfully. "I think maybe he's got a bit of an eye for you. He didn't appear overly happy when I turned up."

"Hardly. I think it more likely he's just got a lot on his mind, wanting this thing to go well tonight."

The request for guests to take their places in the dining room saved her from Sean's disbelieving glance, and she tucked her hand under his elbow with a reluctant smile. It turned into a wince seconds later when she saw their seats were positioned close to the top table. Even worse, she realised she would be directly facing Luke.

Couldn't someone give her a break?

"Hey, what's with this seating plan? I thought we'd be on the top table tonight." Sean gave her a sly wink as he took his seat. "You know it's going to be extremely tiresome if the main man is going to stare disapprovingly at me all night. Takes me back to my school days."

"Don't be ridiculous." Chloe poked him in the ribs.

"You're imagining things." But when she glanced up, it was to find Luke favouring them with an unfriendly gaze. *What had got into him tonight?*

****

Dinner was a lively affair, mainly due to the fact that Sean was an irrepressible comedian. He kept their table in fits of laughter, and Chloe was enjoying herself immensely, but try as she might, she couldn't help glancing across to Luke every so often. Surprisingly, he appeared to have the same difficulty; whenever she looked up, her eyes were met by his questioning gaze.

After the dinner plates were cleared away and the waiting staff were serving coffee, Luke got to his feet and gave an eloquent and touching tribute to Jeff, before outlining his future plans for the Warwick Company Ltd and Hardaker's. As he stood there in his immaculately cut dinner jacket, Chloe couldn't help but be reminded again of the night they first met. She remembered how angry she had been with Lucie, and how he had coaxed her out of her mood, telling her they would never have to see each other again if they found they didn't like each other. That evening had ended in a passionate kiss, an awakening of feelings she had not even known she possessed, and with Luke rejecting her.

In an effort to drive such disconcerting memories from her mind, she tried to concentrate on what he was saying. But focussing on his mouth only served to remind her of how it felt to kiss him, and her own bewildering response to his touch. At that moment, his eyes caught hers and she blushed as though he could read her mind. He paused imperceptibly, his gaze sharpening on the rising colour in her cheeks, before carrying on smoothly, and Chloe listened to the remainder of his speech staring at her hands in her lap, desperately striving to regain her composure.

"You know, if I weren't so hopelessly in love with Rebekah, I rather think I'd marry you," said Sean, considering her carefully as they waltzed slowly around the dance floor after the presentation had given way to a live band.

"Oh really? That's a rather big assumption, Mr. Carter." Her laughter turned into a gasp as he gathered her up in his arms to lift her off her feet and spin her around in a circle.

"Hmmm, our Mr. Warwick didn't like that one little bit. I wonder what would happen if I kissed you?" He dropped a soft, swift kiss just to the left of her mouth before she could protest, and followed it up with a cool, unconcerned glance in Luke's direction as he continued to swing her around the dance floor. "Yep. Definitely not happy. Are you sure there's nothing going on there?"

"Quite sure. I don't know why he keeps looking at you like that, but he's not jealous." Her response was definite. *How could she forget him gently pushing her away on the beach?* "I'm telling you, you're barking up the wrong tree. I mean look at him and then look at me. There's no way he's interested."

Sean stopped mid-turn, and stared at her before holding her at arm's length. "I am looking at you. And any guy would be crazy not to be interested in you."

"Pretty packaging," she muttered, shaking off his restraining hands to slip back into his arms.

"You like him, don't you?" He said softly. It was more of a statement than a question.

"No." Chloe denied it a little too quickly, and

caught his disbelieving smile. She gave a helpless shrug. "Okay, yes. I like him. But it's no good, he...he doesn't feel the same. I know he doesn't." She shrugged again.

"You have to give people a chance." He gently lifted her chin with his finger. They were now standing still, oblivious to the other people dancing around them. "We're not all like Chris, you know."

"So everyone keeps telling me. And I know you're not," she said with a smile. She did know it, but she also knew they weren't the problem; she was.

"Hey, enough of this. We're at a party, we should be dancing." Without warning, Sean caught her around the waist, swinging her backwards over his outstretched arm into a classic Fred Astaire and Ginger Rogers pose, her long hair sweeping the floor in a coppery mass. "Tell me again how wonderful I am, and how Rebekah is lucky to have me."

"I don't think I actually said anything of the sort in the first place." Laughing in surprise, Chloe grasped his shoulders, but felt completely safe in his strong embrace, his face inches above hers. "Very masterful. Okay, you can let me up now. You're causing a scene."

"Nup. Not until you say it." He grinned. "I can stay here all night. You're as light as a feather."

"Okay, okay." She giggled despite herself. "Sean, you are completely wonderful, and Rebekah is very lucky to have you."

"I should think so, too."

Sean made sure she never stopped laughing or dancing all evening, and it was well after midnight when they fell into the taxi and went home to where Rebekah was waiting for them.

****

Chloe spent the rest of the weekend with her friends, walking for miles in the beautiful Yorkshire Dales and rewarding themselves with a hearty meal in the pub at the end of it. After such a stressful week, it was just the distraction she needed, and she went to bed on Sunday evening feeling more rested and relaxed than she had in days. Everything was sorted. She had spoken to John before leaving for the party on Friday, and accepted Mark's offer of the job. All that was left for her to do now was to hand in her notice, put Luke and Chris behind her, and start a new chapter in her life.

With that foremost in her mind on Monday morning, she picked up the envelope sitting on her coffee table and ran her finger across Luke's name, printed in her small, neat handwriting across the middle. She bit her lip, hesitating a moment, before carefully tucking it into her handbag.

How was she going to tell Luke she was leaving?

Chapter Eight

Luke jumped slightly when a soft thump in the outer office told him Chloe had arrived. He had been miles away, unwelcome thoughts and images crowding his mind until he was unable to think clearly. He drew in a breath, rubbing his face with his hands.

God, he was tired.

He'd hardly slept all weekend, wondering where she was and who she was with; she was clearly not at home. Not that it was any of his business, he knew that. But still, it didn't stop the burn of jealousy in the pit of his stomach.

And now this.

He stared with distaste at the large manila envelope sitting on his desk, resisting the urge to pick it up and tear it into tiny pieces.

Keep it focussed, Luke. Keep it business.

He deliberately kept his door shut in an effort to concentrate on the many tasks that awaited his attention, but when she knocked half an hour later, it was almost a relief. Almost.

"Come in."

"Morning, Luke." She smiled breezily, and took her place at the small circular meeting table in the corner of his office where they usually went through his diary for the week.

He noted she was wearing a slightly different outfit today—a white, pin-striped shirt tucked into a tan coloured, mid-calf length A-line skirt, with brown twenties-style lace-up boots. Her hair had been swept to one side to form a long, neat plait that hung down over one shoulder. As quirky as ever, she took his breath away.

After a brief hesitation, he picked up the manila envelope and joined her at the table.

"Did you have a good weekend?" She was fresh-faced and happy, her green eyes shining bright and clear. The antithesis of how he was feeling.

"Yes, thank you." He gestured to her notepad. "Take me through this week."

His response was unusually abrupt, and she blinked in surprise before collecting herself and opening her notepad.

Twenty minutes later and they were done; all his meetings planned, and the outstanding queries dealt with. He'd made it. Chloe began to gather her things together and prepared to leave.

"So, who was he?" The words were out of his mouth before he even knew he was going to speak.

Halfway between standing and sitting, she looked at him in surprise, before sinking back into her seat, and starting to flick through her notebook. "Who? Which meeting…?"

"The handsome joker at the party on Friday. Who was he?" His voice was clipped, and he checked himself with some effort.

She stared at him, confusion clearly written across her face. "Sean? You know who he was. I introduced you."

Luke kept his mouth shut, not trusting himself to speak.

After a long moment during which Chloe's puzzled gaze searched his, she shook her head as if humouring him. "He's a friend."

"A friend?" He gave a snort of disbelief. "A bloody good friend, by the looks of it. He couldn't keep his damn hands off you."

Her jaw dropped open. "Luke, I—"

"God, you fed me a line, didn't you?" He cut her off, pushing himself out of his chair and striding over to the picture window where he stood with his arms folded across his chest. "And like a fool, I fell for it hook, line, and sinker."

When she didn't respond, he turned back to her. She was still sitting in her seat, but her eyes were wide, her knuckles white where they clutched her notebook. His anger abated at her obvious signs of tension, but as his breathing began to slow, his glance fell on the envelope, still lying where he had left it. His mind was immediately filled with those hateful images, evidence of her deception, and his lip curled in disgust.

"All that crap about hating any man to touch you." He gave a short, humourless laugh. "You didn't seem to have any hesitation about kissing me that night on the beach; you clearly didn't mind Sean's hands all over you on Friday; and it sure as hell didn't stop you having an affair with Jefferson."

Chloe recoiled as if she'd been struck, her notebook falling into her lap as her hands flew to her throat. "What are you talking about? I can't believe...you're not making any sense." Her mouth opened and closed as if she were lost for words. "An affair with Niall? Why on earth would you think that?"

"He told me." Luke steeled himself against her obvious distress, reminding himself that she was a fine actress. "You refused to tell me what the fight was about, remember?"

"And you believe him?" Her expressive face betrayed her growing anger.

Good. Because he was bloody angry, too.

"The man embezzles the company, attacks me, and you're willing to take his word over mine? Thanks for the vote of confidence, Luke." She stared at him as if she didn't recognise him. "I did not have an affair with Niall. That's the truth."

"You wouldn't know the truth if it slapped you in the face." Moving back to the coffee table, he picked up the envelope and threw it contemptuously into her lap. Aware that his hands were shaking, he folded his arms and stood waiting for her to open it.

Chloe continued to stare at him, her gaze unwavering, before shaking her head and picking up the envelope. When she drew out the contents, he saw her stiffen, and for what seemed like an eternity, she simply stared at the topmost photograph. Her fingers began to tremble as she slowly shuffled through the rest. He could hear her uneven breathing but could see nothing of her expression, just the top of her bowed head, until she looked up at him. He imagined she could read the contempt in his eyes, because she immediately dropped her gaze.

"Interesting, aren't they?" His stomach was churning. The thought of Chloe with that bastard was enough to make him ill. He didn't need to see graphic proof.

"This isn't me. These aren't real." She looked up at him, her face ashen. "I don't...where did you get them?"

"Jefferson. We had an interesting conversation the other day, he and I." His voice was cold as he walked back to sit behind his desk. "He told me the fight started because he tried to end his affair with you, and that in fact you were blackmailing him, threatening to tell his wife about the two of you if he finished it."

"And you believe him?"

"I didn't," he admitted with a shrug, before gesturing to the photographs still clutched in her hands. "But then those photographs arrived over the weekend, and I got to thinking. Thinking about that night on the beach, about Sean...and I believe you even said yourself the fight was over something personal?"

"Not that." Her voice was little more than a whisper. "It wasn't about that."

"Then perhaps you'd care to give me your version of events? Come on, I'm dying to hear what you're going to dream up next. I love a good story."

"No!" Chloe shot to her feet, angry colour flooding her face as she strode towards him and threw the photographs on his desk. "You can go and take a running jump. I don't need to explain myself to you. You clearly want to believe the worst, so why should I waste my breath? These photographs are obviously photoshopped or whatever it is you call it. But go ahead, believe what you like...and you know what?" She was trembling from head to foot. "You've just made this so much easier for me."

Luke took a shaky breath when she stalked out of the office, only to return moments later with her phone, and a plain white envelope which she threw down on the desk in front of him. He recognised his name written in her handwriting.

"My resignation letter. I'm giving you one month's notice."

His heart was racing in his chest, but he met her gaze steadily and she returned it without flinching, before finally looking down and tapping through various screens on her phone. She was clearly searching for something, and he frowned. Now what?

"I never lied to you, Luke." Her voice was quiet and clear. She leaned forward to carefully place her phone on top of the envelope. "I've spent the last year trying to convince myself that I didn't deserve this, that it wasn't my fault."

He glanced down at the phone…and the bottom fell out of his world.

It was a photograph of Chloe, although she was barely recognisable. Her left eye was bruised and swollen shut; a long, ugly graze ran across her cheek; and her lip was bloody and split.

Nausea rose in his stomach, and he swallowed with difficulty. When she spoke again, it was all he could do to stop himself from covering his ears with his hands so he didn't have to listen.

"He told me I'd never find anyone else who would put up with me, who would love me. That I should be grateful for him. I left him the night he did that. I still don't know if I was brave or stupid, but I'm determined to prove him wrong. To prove my mother wrong."

Luke was unable to take his eyes from the awful photograph on the phone, but her words burned into him.

"You know, for a little while there I thought you were different. I thought you saw something in me that no-one else did, that you believed I was worth something." She shook her head when he eventually looked up to meet her gaze and saw the tears shining there. "But it doesn't matter now."

"I'm worth more than this." She reached across to pick up the phone, and gestured towards the photographs. "And I'm worth more than those...those pictures. I don't care what you think anymore."

She turned and walked unsteadily from the room, closing the door softly behind her, leaving Luke staring after her in grim silence. His gaze dropped to the photographs scattered across his desk, and he felt a burning rage bubbling up inside. Before he knew what he was doing, in one swift movement he swept them to the floor.

His anger dissipated as quickly as it had appeared, and he leaned his elbows on the desk, pressing the heels of his hands against his eyes as he swallowed down the acidic bile at the back of his throat. His stomach gave a sickening lurch, and he staggered to his feet and across to the window, opening it wide and drawing in huge, deep breaths to try to stem the nausea rolling over him.

The cool breeze soothed his burning face, and he focussed on the busy harbour across the way from him. People going about their everyday business, completely oblivious to the angry exchanges that had taken place behind the plain exterior of the Hardaker building. His gaze rose to the houses crammed together on the harbour side, row upon row of houses stacked against the sides of the cliff, and he wondered what secrets lay behind all those other windows and doors.

How had he got it so wrong?

Chloe was a victim of domestic abuse. A survivor.

He gripped the edges of the window frame as he tried to comprehend the enormity of that information. Everything made so much more sense now—the conciliatory way she had responded sometimes to a flippant remark; her hasty retreat around the desk when he had moved towards her after Niall's attack.

And he'd accused her of lying to him, of having an affair and blackmailing Niall.

Luke pinched the bridge of his nose as he returned to his desk, ashamed by his lack of control, at the way he had allowed his emotions to get the better of him. But worse than that, he'd allowed Niall to play him.

Suddenly close to tears, he slumped forward on the desk to rest his forehead on his arms. His grandfather would have been so disappointed in him.

Always two sides to a story, Luke; you don't know anything until you've heard both.

"I wish you were here, Gramps," he whispered. "I don't know what's happening to me."

The faint bleeping from his laptop reminded him that he was due for a meeting in ten minutes. He slowly straightened up from the desk, passing a hand over his face, and made a valiant effort to clear his head, to concentrate on the task in hand. After a brief hesitation, he gathered up the photographs and shoved them into the shredding machine before pouring himself a strong coffee. The liquid scalded his throat as he stared at the door to the outer office. Was Chloe there, preparing for the meeting, or had she walked out? He couldn't blame her if she had.

****

Although he didn't know it, Chloe was also sitting at her seat and struggling to organise her thoughts.

How could he believe she was capable of lying? Of blackmailing Niall? Was that truly how he saw her?

She bit back a sob as her anger evaporated. No, it wasn't how he saw her; that was, it hadn't been until he'd seen those photographs. And how could she blame him for that? Hadn't she thought the same thing about John, when she'd found that folder in Niall's cabinet? My God, how many others did Niall have hidden away, just in case?

She stared down at her hands, absently picking at the edge of her fingernail. She had lied to Luke; told him it didn't matter what he thought anymore. But it did matter; it mattered so much. That was the only reason she had shown him the photograph of her the day after she had left Chris. Not because she wanted his pity, but to make him understand why she said and did the things she did, to prove she hadn't lied.

She heard voices coming up the corridor, and she straightened, her heart sinking when she belatedly remembered Luke's meeting that morning. A quick look in her mirror compact gave her slight reassurance, and she pasted on the best smile she could manage as she went through to the boardroom.

Making small talk with the board members as they arrived was something of a trial, and Chloe hoped no-one would notice her rather vague and inane responses. She would usually tap on Luke's door to let him know they were ready to start the meeting, but today he didn't wait for her and simply came through at ten o'clock sharp to take his place at the table.

Pouring coffee and tea, she clutched the pot a little

tighter to control the slight tremor in her hands, smiling automatically as someone made a rather lame joke about being sweet enough as they pushed the sugar bowl aside.

"Are you all right, Chloe? You look a bit pale." One of the older members of the board caught her eye as she passed him a cup of tea. She saw Luke's head snap in her direction, and deliberately turned her face away from him.

"I'm fine, thank you." She gave a brief, reassuring smile, before circulating copies of the agenda and minutes from the previous meeting.

Head down and scribbling furiously as the meeting began, it was something of a relief to be able to concentrate on taking the minutes and to have a genuine reason for ignoring everyone else in the room. That didn't stop her from being aware of Luke's rigid posture; he was clearly as tense as she was.

When the meeting drew to a close two hours later, she gratefully retreated to her office, breathing a sigh of relief, safe in the knowledge that Luke would be busy with meetings for the rest of the day.

****

"Oh, for heaven's sake!"

Beads scattered across the worktable as the thin wire earring rod slipped from Chloe's jewellery pliers. Growling in frustration, she scooped up the beads and carefully dropped them into one of the little plastic drawers of her bead box. It was no good. She couldn't concentrate on her jewellery making, not after this morning, no matter how much she needed to build up her stock ready for the shop.

Sitting back in her chair, she gazed through the

window, allowing the view to calm her unsettled mood. The early evening sun still shone with surprising warmth and, as the soft breeze came in through the open window, she closed her eyes and lifted her face to breathe in the salty air. After a while, the breeze grew stronger, lifting the curtains, and stirring the shells and wind chimes hanging in the garden, the melodious chords urging her outside, and she smiled. Yes, she needed fresh air.

The path was warm on her bare feet as she walked through the kitchen garden and down to the patio area at the very bottom. Two walls built at right angles created a shelter from the perpetual winds that blew in off the sea and, on a sunny afternoon like this, it was a lovely little suntrap. Rose filled trellises covered the walled area, filling the little space with their heady scent, and Chloe breathed in their soothing fragrance as she sank onto the shaded garden swing, turning sideways to draw up her legs and rest her head on the back of the long, cushioned seat.

She was just drifting off to sleep when Jasper began to bark and scampered down the path to disappear around the side of the house. Chloe blinked sleepily; she hadn't heard a car, so it couldn't be anyone calling to see her. Jasper must be hearing things.

"Hello, girl. Is Chloe around the back? Is that why no-one's answering the door?"

Her stomach dropped when she saw Luke appear, bending to stroke Jasper as she leaped up at him in delight while he walked towards the patio, for the moment unaware of Chloe's presence. She steeled herself for yet another encounter with him.

He looked up and saw her. "Hey."

She didn't answer, just concentrated on keeping her expression neutral, on making sure he couldn't tell her heart was racing.

He sat down on the wicker chair opposite and met her gaze. He had changed into blue jeans and a navy t-shirt. The traces of sand on his trainers explained why she hadn't heard a car; he'd clearly walked across the beach.

"Chloe, I…" He stopped, and leaned forwards to rest his forearms on his knees. "I don't know where to start. What I said…what I thought…was unforgivable. After everything you've been through…"

The usually cool, confident man was suddenly stripped bare. She had never seen him so unsure, but there was no doubting his sincerity, and she responded instinctively, turning towards him, and swinging her legs to the floor.

"It's not unforgivable. You didn't know. And those photographs, the things I did—"

"Don't you dare," he said softly. "Don't you dare suggest it was okay for me to say those things, to imply that anything you did somehow justified what I thought or said to you."

"Chloe…" He frowned and rubbed his forehead. "I don't have any excuses, not really. I'd had Niall bloody whispering in my ear the week before, then you turned up to the party with Sean and looking happier than I'd ever seen you, and the following day those photos arrived on my doorstep. It sent me in a spin. And all I can say is that I'm sorry. I'm not trying to justify what I said, I'm trying to explain why I said it."

Chloe stared him, confused by his explanation.

"You were angry because you thought I'd lied to you?"

"Yes, to an extent." He gave a crooked smile. "But if I'm being completely honest, I was mainly just jealous as hell."

She shook her head. He wasn't making any sense. "Jealous of what?"

"Jealous of whom, you mean. I was jealous of the guy who made you look so happy. Sean."

She flinched and shot to her feet. "I don't know what kind of game you're playing, Luke, but I don't want to play anymore. Please will you just go?"

He stood up slowly, looking bewildered. "I'm not playing games."

"Really?" She looked away in frustration. Was he really going to make her spell it out?

"Okay, so tell me then. Why were you jealous of Sean?" Chloe stood with her head on one side as if humouring him. *Don't say it. Please don't lie.*

"Because I wanted to be the one dancing with you, holding your hand…kissing you."

"No! Why would you say that? Why all this…this lying about being jealous? I don't understand why you would come here and say you're sorry, and then lie to me about something like this."

"I'm not lying," he said quietly.

She gave an inarticulate cry of frustration, her hands clenched into fists. "But you are! You used me. Do you think I don't know that you used me? That you went to the Ball specifically because you knew I worked for the company you were buying?"

She stepped back quickly when he reached for her, clearly shocked by her outburst.

"You weren't jealous of Sean or Niall. This

154

morning, you accused me of lying to you, but when have you ever told me the truth?"

She gave a scornful laugh. "That night on the beach, you couldn't push me away fast enough when I kissed you. And the night of the storm, you held me in your arms and did nothing, just put me in your bed and left me alone. So much for wanting to kiss me, for being jealous of other men. In fact, you even spelled it out to me in the kitchen the following day. You're not looking for a relationship, remember? You warned me off in no uncertain terms. Not that you needed to."

Her anger dissipated suddenly, and her voice dropped to a whisper. "I know you don't want me, Luke Warwick, so why are you lying?"

She stared at him through her tears, and didn't move when he stepped towards her slowly, as if expecting her to turn and run. He was pale beneath his tan and he took a deep, steadying breath.

"That night we first met, I wanted to kiss you so badly. And then you kissed me, and it was…it was amazing. But you were angry and upset, and kissing me for the wrong reasons. That was why I pulled away." He grimaced. "The night of the storm was the longest night of my entire life. You have no idea how much I wanted to join you in that bed. But that wouldn't have been right either, you know that. You were exhausted, you were hurt and, aside from all that, you confused the hell out of me."

He dragged a hand through his hair. "Chloe, I've wanted you from the first moment I saw you, but what I said in the kitchen was true; I'm not in a position to offer you anything. And yet at the same time, I can't seem to stay away from you and it's tearing me apart."

He lifted her chin until she was forced to meet his gaze, and she drew in a sharp breath at the vulnerability she saw there. "You tie me in knots. I've never lied to you...about anything."

"You knew I worked for Hardaker's..."

"We talked about this. I didn't know until you told me that lunchtime. I didn't go to the Ball with any ulterior motives, and I'm not even sure what motives you think I might have had." He shook his head. "What do you think I might have gained? When you told me about Hardaker's, it threw me, you know that. All I could think was that you would be working for me and I really didn't want you to work for me."

He gave a lopsided grin at her look of surprise. "I didn't want you to work for me because I never mix work and pleasure. And when I thought of you, it was definitely with pleasure in mind. So, yes it threw me when you told me who you worked for, and no I didn't tell you I had bought Hardaker's, but...that was the only reason. I just didn't manage to think on my feet quickly enough."

She wanted to believe him so badly. He took a step closer, cupping her face as he bent his head to kiss her, and she held her breath, closing her eyes, fully expecting him to pull away immediately. His mouth brushed hers with a butterfly kiss, and it was almost a relief when, as expected, he lifted his head. But instead of pulling away, he stayed close, his lips millimetres from hers.

"Kiss me." His eyes shone with understanding...and desire, and it gave her the confidence to lift her lips to his, to inch that little bit closer and, as his lips caught hers once more, it felt like coming home. She had never experienced a kiss with such tenderness, such care. With Chris, it had always been about sex, and he had been all too eager to point out her shortcomings. Luke's kisses sent her reeling, delicious sensations tingling through her body when he pulled her in close, his hand burning the small of her back.

"Chloe MacGregor." His lips curved in a smile against hers when he said her name softly.

She giggled, ducking her head to the floor, overcome with a sudden shyness. "Luke Warwick."

She had no idea how long they had been standing there, kissing, but her lips tingled, and she felt rather weak in the knees.

Clasping her hand in his, Luke pulled her to the garden swing, kissing her palm as they sat down, and she leaned into him, dropping her head onto his shoulder. *Was this really happening?* Her heart felt as if it would burst with happiness.

"Come on. Spit it out."

His voice held a trace of laughter when he broke the companionable silence, his fingers tracing lazy swirls along her arm. Her mind had begun to wander as she replayed their conversation, and he must have recognised the change in her mood.

She lifted her head and hesitated before speaking, reluctant to bring the subject up again. "I meant what I said earlier, about understanding why you reacted like you did." She felt him stiffen beside her, and lifted a hand to stop his protests. "I understand because I know how I reacted when I saw similar photographs. Luke, there are others…other photographs of people from Hardaker's. People who were blackmailed."

He frowned in surprise and then, after a moment's pause, "John." He spoke with absolute certainty. "My God, that's why he retired, isn't it? The bloody fool; why didn't he tell me?"

"He couldn't. He wasn't willing to risk hurting his wife, Sarah." Chloe lifted her shoulders uneasily. "You know what people are like, all that speculation and gossip. But the reason I'm telling you is because John said Niall produced those photographs immediately when he confronted him about the fraud. Niall didn't go away and fake the photographs. He already had them."

She saw comprehension dawn in Luke's eyes, and he smiled grimly. "Insurance. He's a thorough man, I'll give him that; he would want to be sure he had every base covered. You think he's got those photographs for everyone in Hardaker's?"

"I'm not sure about everyone." She wrinkled her nose. "Maybe those most likely to present a risk to him. Not sure why I would be on that list, though."

"Anyone working with you for five minutes would know how thorough and sharp you are." Luke smoothed her hair back behind her ear. "I'll inform the police; they've already got his laptop and are searching his house. I'll go through his office."

"They were hidden in the back of his filing cabinet. I'm not sure if he will have had a chance to move them." Chloe shifted uncomfortably. "I made copies of the photographs and the letter blackmailing John, and taped them to the underneath of my desk drawer until I figured out what to do."

"That's it, isn't it?" His gaze sharpened in realisation. "That's why he attacked you. He knew you had found the photographs."

She nodded, dropping her gaze to where her hand was still clasped in his. "At first, he thought I'd been passing information to you about him, but then I confronted him about blackmailing John. Looking back, it was a stupid thing to do. What happened was my fault, I should have backed down."

"It wasn't stupid. It was actually pretty brave." Luke waited until she met his gaze. "And it wasn't your fault. None of it was your fault."

His voice was even more gravelly than usual, and his fingers trembled as they gently traced along her cheekbone and down to her lips. She knew he wasn't just talking about Niall, but about Chris too. She had heard it so often; from Rebekah, from Sean, and from herself but, somehow, she had never truly believed it. Today though, when Luke said it, something shifted, something eased, and her breathing hitched a little as a flicker of hope unfurled inside her. He bent his head to kiss her—a kiss so careful, so gentle, it was as if he were afraid she might break. Maybe, just maybe, she could start to believe it.

Chapter Nine

Luke could hear Chloe's voice as he walked up to the front door and, seeing it was half open, he knocked softly and went in. He was eager to see her. They had agreed to keep things casual between them while she still worked for him, and as a result the last two weeks had seemed endless. But Friday had been Chloe's last day, and having spent yesterday with his brother, he was now looking forward to spending some time with her.

"…Mum, there's really nothing to tell but…he's nice and…I'm happy." She was standing by the window, and speaking into her mobile phone. She glanced up when he entered and gave him a distracted smile, falling silent while she listened and blushed in response to whatever her mother had said. "Well…like I said, it's early days. We haven't…"

Not wishing to intrude, Luke caught her eye.

"Coffee?" he mouthed.

When she nodded, he went through to the kitchen, flicked on the kettle, and leaned back against the counter. He liked Chloe's little cottage. It reflected the quirky, mischievous girl he had seen dancing and whirling down on the beach, unaware of his gaze; the one who had teased him in his kitchen following the storm; the girl who had a penchant for seashells, which were everywhere he looked—and for Edinburgh rock.

He gazed thoughtfully around her kitchen. Despite it being almost clinically clean, it was filled with personality. Scarlet red geraniums were crammed onto the windowsill, their leaves entwined with the lengths of seashells hanging from the curtain rail. Numerous small paintings—unframed and torn straight from the pad—were pinned haphazardly to the noticeboard. He peered closer, and saw they were studies of the local landscape, all signed with a barely noticeable CM; Chloe MacGregor. Shaking his head in wonder, he turned away and, as he did so, his eye was caught by the photographs pinned to the fridge by yet more shells, magnetic ones this time. There was Chloe mugging up to the camera with a blonde-haired woman, large glasses of wine held up as they grinned at whoever was taking the picture. The next photograph was again of Chloe, but this time she was down on the beach and hugging Jasper, then still a puppy. It must have been taken last winter because she was wrapped in a quilted jacket, gloves, and scarf, and her nose was decidedly pink, but he thought she had never looked more beautiful. He ran a gentle finger across the photograph.

This was a girl full of warmth and laughter, who had so much love to give. And yet, this was also a girl who had sat at his kitchen table and calmly informed him she didn't believe in love. He shook his head silently, his eyes still on the photographs. She was wrong. It wasn't that she didn't believe in love, it was more that she believed she was unlovable. The thought of whoever or whatever had made her feel like that twisted in his stomach like a knife. It was as far from the truth as anyone could get. Chloe deserved to love and be loved and cherished. But he worried that he wasn't and couldn't be that man. He couldn't give her what she needed, which was stability and commitment. And yet here he was, almost paralysed by an overwhelming need to be with her. It confused and frightened him.

She was still on the phone when he returned to the living room with the coffee. She smiled her thanks and then visibly tensed in response to something her mother must have said. She turned away from him.

"Why can't you just be happy that I'm happy?" A pause. "Well, thanks for your support, Mum."

She threw her phone onto the chair beside her without turning around, and he saw her shoulders lift as she took in a deep breath.

"Hey." He moved across the room and folded his arms around her. After a brief hesitation, she leaned back into him. "You okay?"

She nodded uncertainly.

"Want to talk about it?"

"No," she said after a pause, and then turned to give him a bright smile as she brushed past him and went into the kitchen. "I've made us a light tea if you're interested."

****

"Bye."

"You on the phone again?" Luke teased, as he walked through to the living room after washing up the tea dishes.

"No, why?"

"Oh. I thought I heard you saying goodbye to someone." He looked at her quizzically.

"I did. I was saying goodbye to Steven Hadshaw."

Chloe pointed to the newsreader on the television, and who was now gathering up his papers as the credits scrolled across the screen.

"Right." A slow smile creased his face. "You always speak to the newsreader then, do you?"

"Well, yes, don't you?" He loved the way she looked at him as if he had suggested something out of the ordinary. "It's only polite to respond when he says good morning, goodbye, or whatever."

"But you know he can't hear you, right?"

"You can laugh at me all you want, Luke Warwick." She pulled a face at him. "Okay then, who is he talking to, when he says good morning and good night?"

A pause. "The viewers. The public."

"Exactly. And who am I?"

"Okay, you're right. You're a viewer." He held up his hands in defeat. He couldn't argue with her logic.

"Yes. I'm a viewer. He is speaking to me, and it would therefore be very rude if I didn't respond when he wishes me a good morning."

Luke slipped his hands around her waist and smiled down at her. "Don't you ever change, Chloe MacGregor."

Settling down on the sofa to watch the television, he could feel her gaze, and he smiled without taking his eyes from the screen. "Have I suddenly grown two heads?"

He glanced across at her then and saw her blushing.

"I was just thinking." She picked at a loose thread on her skirt. "You said some really nice things at my leaving lunch on Friday."

He gave a soft laugh, and frowned. "And that surprised you? Did you expect me to say something awful?"

"No, of course not." She smiled. "It's just…the last two weeks have flown by and, although I'm sad to be leaving everyone, I'm really excited to be starting my new job."

"As you should be." He couldn't help but tease her. "And as you've only worked two weeks of your notice, you were clearly desperate to leave."

"You said I could take my holiday—"

"I was joking." He shook his head in amused exasperation. "Two weeks of keeping my distance from you, of not being able to touch you or kiss you, was more than long enough."

She nodded and looked as if she were about to say something else, but fell silent, and it was his turn to watch her as she turned her gaze to the television with a troubled expression.

"Come on, let's go down to the beach before we lose the light." He got to his feet and turned to pull her to her feet. "There's a bottle of wine in the fridge."

****

Chloe spread the blanket over the sand and stretched out, lifting her face to the sinking sun while Luke threw sticks for Jasper. The warm weather was holding for the moment, but it wouldn't be long before the sea breeze brought with it the promise of autumn. After a quarter of an hour, it became obvious that Jasper wasn't going to tire of this game and Luke, with a final hefty throw into the ocean, flung himself down beside Chloe with a groan.

"Your dog is nuts."

"She sure is." Lying on her back with her eyes closed, Chloe smiled.

"You okay?" He rolled over onto his elbow to look down at her. "I know I wasn't around yesterday, but Friday was a big day for you."

"I'm okay."

"You know, Scott told me I should offer you a promotion; he said I should fight to keep you."

"Did he? I like Scott. He's a nice man." A smile curved her mouth, but she didn't open her eyes.

"Oh yes? How nice?" Without giving her a chance to respond, he leaned down and gave her a lingering kiss.

"Not that nice," she smiled against his lips. "And I'm really okay. Thank you."

"Good." He kissed her again briefly before reaching across to open the bottle of wine, pouring her a glass and handing it to her when she sat up. "To new beginnings, then."

She glanced at him quickly with a slightly quizzical expression. "New beginnings."

She rested her head on his shoulder as they sat side by side on the blanket in easy silence, and watched as the light began to fade and twinkling stars gradually appeared in the dusky sky. Jasper appeared perfectly content to race around the beach, absorbed in her own little games.

"I gather you told your mother you were seeing someone." He said at last.

She stiffened, and lifted her head to take a swallow of wine. "Is that what we're doing? Are we seeing each other?"

She looked up at him, her gaze searching his. "I'm

not really sure what we're doing, Luke. I know you don't want anything serious, and you've made it clear you don't want commitment, but you know, that's nothing new. I'm not—"

"Don't say that," he cut in fiercely. "That's not it. That's not it at all. I'm terrified of hurting you. I want you so badly, but I'll end up hurting you. You don't need a fling, you need someone to love you, to be with you forever."

To his complete surprise, she started to laugh. "How do you know what I need? What I want? You think you know me, but you don't. Not really. You have no idea what I need."

"I know you are beautiful and kind and good. And you deserve to be loved."

"I'm not asking for forever, Luke. I'm not even sure forever exists," she said softly. "But I do know that you make me feel things I've never felt before, in so many different ways. You make me feel whole, you make me feel like a woman, and I never, ever thought I would feel that."

His heart was thumping so loudly he was barely able to hear her soft words, but he did hear them. "Chloe…"

"I'm afraid too. I'm frightened that I'll never feel again the way I feel when you kiss me."

He closed his eyes, desperate to take her into his arms, but needing her to understand him first. After a moment, he turned his gaze to the calm ocean in front of them, his arms resting on his knees.

"I was twelve years old when my parents split up. We were a close-knit family, not overly demonstrative but, you know, calm, quiet, and happy. It seemed to come out of nowhere; there were no arguments, no big blow-up or anything. Just one day, my dad sat me down and said he was sorry, but he had to leave. And that's what he did; he left." Luke swallowed hard. He had never spoken about this to anyone except his grandfather. "My brother was away at university, and Mum…well, she took it badly, couldn't cope at all, and had a complete breakdown. She didn't leave the bedroom for months, but I could hear her crying; huge, awful sobs. It seemed like it was all day, every day; the sound of her agony terrified me. I'll never forget it." He passed a hand over his face.

"My aunt came to stay with us. She was Mum's sister and, of course, she took her side, but the things she said about Dad were awful. I couldn't bear it. I loved my father. I loved Mum, too, and it tore me apart to see her so broken. But to hear them talk like that, I couldn't understand it. It didn't fit with the man I knew."

Chloe remained silent, but gently placed her hand on his arm as he dug his fingers deep into the sand beside him.

"I think my grandfather saved me that summer. He was a shipbuilder, and had a small dinghy that he would take me out in. We would spend whole days fishing out on the sea in the holidays." He smiled at the memory. "I remember asking him how my dad could just leave us like that, how he could hurt Mum so badly. Gramps was so…I don't know, so calm about it, particularly considering Mum was his daughter. He was very careful about not laying the blame solely with my father. He told me they wanted different things. Mum wanted a settled, happy family, but Dad was a restless spirit, always had been. He'd tried so hard to settle down, working nine to five to give us the stability Mum needed, but by doing that, he was denying who he really was."

He glanced down at Chloe and gave her a quick smile. "Gramps was very like you. He had a strong moral compass, a sense of what was right. He talked to me about taking responsibility for my actions, to understand that everyone is different, warning me about how dangerous it is to assume the person you fall in love with will want the same things in life as you."

He fell silent for a moment, digging deep in the sand before holding out his hand and watching the grains blow away on the wind as it slipped through his fingers.

"He was an amazing man, my grandfather. That summer was the best time of my life, despite the awful situation at home. I feel as if I learnt all my life lessons in those few months." He laughed softly. "I'm making it sound as if he spent all day every day lecturing me, but it wasn't like that. We spent a lot of those hours in the boat in complete silence. But over the course of that summer, I learnt so much. I owe him pretty much everything.

"Mum eventually found herself again, met someone else, and ended up happily married to my step-dad—and he's great, much more suited to her. But the sound of her sobbing into the night as I tried to get to sleep has stayed with me." He shook his head. "I don't ever want to be the reason someone hurts so badly."

Chloe leaned against him, linking her arm through his. "Do you ever see your dad?"

"I see him once or twice a year. He's still travelling, living the nomadic life, but you know, he's happy. And in the end, that's all I want for him." Luke smiled at last. "I know he carried an awful lot of guilt for a long time. He did love Mum, but he couldn't live the life she needed. When she remarried and he could see how happy she was, I think a huge weight left him. He's never remarried and, to be honest, I don't think he ever will."

"I can see why you bought Hardaker's. It was because of your grandfather."

He leaned across to kiss the top of her head. "Partly."

"I'm not asking for forever, Luke." She said quietly.

"I don't want to hurt you." He closed his eyes, but opened them in surprise when he felt her fingers tighten around his arm.

"I'm tougher than I look."

He pulled back a little and she lifted her head when he ran a gentle finger over her brow to smooth the frown that had appeared there, tracing a path down along her cheekbones, along her jawline, and to her lips. As she lifted her gaze to his, he dropped his head to kiss her, pulling her down beside him on the blanket. He shifted slightly so he could deepen the kiss, running his tongue along the edge of her lips, and was rewarded when she drew in a soft breath. When she tentatively met his tongue with her own, he felt a stab of desire burn through him and he groaned with the effort required to retain his self-control, to take it slowly. He trailed his hand along her collarbone, down into the soft valley between her breasts, delighting in hearing the soft moan that escaped her lips, and down along her hip to cup her behind and bring her closer against him.

Moving his body over hers, he brushed the hair from her face as he kissed her eyes, her mouth, the hollows of her neck, and down to the soft swell of her breast. His breath caught when she arched against him and pulled him closer. It was getting harder to remember his reasons for not taking things further but, despite his desperate need for her, he shifted his weight and rolled onto his side.

"We need to stop." He took a deep breath and dragged a hand through his hair. "We need to stop or…I'm not going to be able to stop."

She met his gaze directly and, to his surprise, he saw her lips twitch mischievously before she deliberately drew his head down to her mouth. Unable to resist, he lay back on the blanket, pulling her with him without breaking their kiss until she was lying on top of him. She automatically straddled him, gasping against his mouth when he moved under her and, as she began to move with him, he groaned at the exquisite sensations shooting through his body. It was too much to bear, and he gripped her waist fiercely, forcing her to keep still. "Don't, Chloe. I can't…"

Her hair tumbled like a waterfall around their faces as she leaned down to whisper against his lips. "Don't you want to?"

"God, yes. But I don't have anything with me…"

"It's okay." She hesitated, colour rising in her cheeks. "I've…got it sorted."

His breathing was coming in ragged gasps as he fought to remain in control. "Are you sure?"

She reached for his belt buckle as his hands

caressed her thighs, her soft cries echoing across the beach before fading away into nothing on the cool, night breeze.

Chapter Ten

Safe and warm within his embrace, snug under the blanket that Luke had tucked around them, Chloe cuddled closer against him. She could hear his heartbeat—now returned to normal—thudding in his chest, and a contented smile curved her lips.

"Are you okay?" he whispered against the top of her head, his arms tightening around her.

She nodded and buried her face in his neck. "It was…I had no idea it could be like that."

He tucked a wayward strand of hair behind her ear and, when she automatically lifted her head, he captured her mouth in a soft, tender kiss. "You are amazing, Chloe MacGregor. And don't let anyone ever tell you different."

She shook her head against his chest. "Not everyone would agree with you."

"Are things difficult with your mum?" His voice was hesitant, as if unsure about broaching the subject.

She didn't respond for a long moment. "No, things aren't difficult. She's just…she hasn't got…" She broke off. How did she explain her relationship with her mother? In the end, she decided to start from the beginning—as she knew it.

"Mum isn't a particularly open person, and she never speaks about my father. All I know is what I've tried to piece together from things she and my grandparents have said, and from speaking to Sandy— one of the friends she grew up with. I guess I've only got one side of the story, but…with the way Mum is…well, I don't know."

She sat up, shuffling close as Luke sat up, too, and secured the blanket around them. "Mum was really pretty when she was younger; she still is, to be honest. My grandparents were apparently quite Victorian in their ways, very strict about dating, and definitely no sex before marriage. You know the type of thing. I'm not saying they weren't loving parents, it's just that they were distant and a bit old-fashioned."

"Mum and her friend Sandy used to sneak out to go to one of the nightclubs in town, but once she'd turned eighteen my grandparents couldn't really stop her anymore. Anyway, she met Johnny, who according to Sandy, was this gorgeous, streetwise twenty-year-old who was infatuated by Mum. She fell for him straight away and, at first, he found her "no sex before marriage" thing amusing. After a while though, I guess it grew a bit thin, and they ended up arguing about it until eventually he split up with her. He didn't waste any time in turning to, and sleeping with Sandy, which broke my mother's heart. It didn't last, though; he'd got what he wanted and just moved on to the next girl. But, according to Sandy, he was still obsessed with Mum— the one girl he couldn't have, until finally he proposed to her. Mum was thrilled. Johnny was all she had ever wanted, and now he'd asked her to marry him; he must really love her. They were married within three months, but I'm guessing you must know it wasn't a happy ever after."

Luke's arm tightened around her, and she leaned into him.

"I don't think the wedding night went very well. Mum wanted everything to be perfect, but apparently Johnny spent most of the night in the bar getting wrecked before finally going up to their room. Anyway, he left the next morning while she was still asleep, and she never saw him again."

Luke drew in a sharp breath of surprise, leaning away slightly to look at her. "She never saw him again? What, never?"

She gave a half smile, shrugging her shoulders. "Apparently not. Mum hadn't spoken to Sandy since Johnny had slept with her, but when her friend found out what he did, she went straight round to see Mum and they made it up. They'd both been taken in by him. Mum never talked about what happened on their wedding night, but two months later, she found out she was pregnant. Eventually, she managed to find out where Johnny was and wrote to him to let him know, but he wrote back and said he wasn't interested and wanted a divorce. She never heard from him again, and she hasn't ever allowed another man close since."

Chloe shifted in Luke's warm embrace, feeling secure and protected. "I know Mum and I have our moments, but I do know it's only because she doesn't want me to go through what she did."

He didn't say anything for a moment. "I can understand how bitter your mother must feel. What your father—"

"He's not my father. He doesn't deserve that title."

Luke acknowledged her vehement denial with a nod and a humourless smile. "You're right...what

Johnny did was truly awful."

He hesitated before hooking a finger under her chin and lifting her face to his. "But what your mother has done to you, is still doing to you, is equally so. You've grown up believing that somehow, you're not worthy of a man's love, that you have nothing to offer. Nothing could be further from the truth."

"Maybe." She frowned, avoiding his gaze, before lifting her shoulders and laughing softly. "Well, I wasn't expecting us to be baring our souls tonight. I imagine some people would call this therapy."

A sharp bark made them both jump, and they turned as one to see Jasper bouncing around them impatiently, having clearly decided she had been ignored for long enough.

"I think she's trying to tell us it's time to go home." Chloe reluctantly left the sanctuary of Luke's arms to kneel beside him and shrug into her jacket.

"Agreed." He squinted in the near darkness. "And while I hate to sound like the MD of a shipbuilding company, I really do have some paperwork to finish before tomorrow."

"Do you want to do that at mine, or are you going back to yours?" She blushed, a sudden shyness stealing over her.

He grimaced, and closed his eyes. "Every fibre in my body is telling me to come with you back to yours, but I know if I do that, I definitely won't get any work done."

She giggled in surprised delight at his obvious reluctance. "Okay. I'll say good night then."

She leaned across and kissed him, smiling when he drew in a quick breath as she deliberately pushed him back onto the blanket. His arms closed around her and he rolled over, pinning her beneath him.

"Enough, you little witch," he grinned, before getting to his feet and pulling her with him. "Would you like to have dinner with me tomorrow night?"

She pretended to consider his invitation; her head cocked to one side. "Hmm, would I like to have dinner with you...let's see...yes, please. Shall I cook, seeing as I have a whole week off before I start my new job?"

"That sounds good. So, what are your plans for tomorrow? A lie-in and lazy day?"

"Oh, no. I'm a morning person, so I'll be up bright and early. A walk on the beach with Jas, and then I've got some serious work to do with to get my jewellery stock ready."

He nodded at her enthusiastic response, before gathering up the blanket, empty wine bottle, and glasses. "Well, I guess I'll see you tomorrow night then."

"Good night. I had a lovely time tonight. Thank you." She stood on tiptoe to kiss his cheek, but instead he pulled her against him and kissed her; a hard, passionate kiss that left her weak at the knees.

"Good night, Chloe. Sleep well."

****

Not for the first time, Luke stood on the beach, watching Chloe's progress as she followed Jasper up the cliff path to her cottage, stopping briefly at the top to wave before she disappeared from view.

They had crossed a line tonight and, while she had reassured him she wasn't looking for commitment, he knew that was what she truly craved, even if she didn't know it herself. And right now, his own feelings for her ran far deeper than he'd ever known. He wanted to spend every waking moment with her, to cherish and care for her, to make love to her. But his father's blood ran through his veins. What if he suddenly found he wanted to escape, to leave everything behind, including Chloe?

The thought terrified him.

He turned away from the cliffs and began slowly walking across the beach to his own path. But what if he didn't want to escape? What if his feelings only got stronger? He had also inherited his grandfather's genes; and the love his grandparents had shared, they had taken to their grave. What was it Chloe had said? *I'm not looking for forever*. Maybe all they could do was take it one day at a time.

****

Still dressed in her nightshirt, Chloe stood at the kitchen window, nibbling toast, and sipping her coffee. It was just gone seven o'clock in the morning, and she shivered a little in the cool air coming through the kitchen door, open as usual to allow Jasper to run in and out while her mistress finished her breakfast. Lost in thought, Chloe gazed through the window without really seeing the garden.

It was odd to wake up and realise she wouldn't be working with Luke anymore, that there was no guarantee she would see him every day. That last Friday had been bittersweet, filled with lots of presents, kisses, and hugs from her work colleagues, but she had left the office alone and returned to her cottage, spending Saturday working on her jewellery, knowing that Luke had gone away Friday night and wouldn't return until Sunday. He had said he was visiting his brother, and she had no reason to doubt him. And yet, worry settled like ice in her stomach.

They'd seen each other a couple of times over the last two weeks, and had gone out to dinner the previous weekend, but she knew he wanted to keep things fairly low key while she was still working for him. Now, though, there was nothing to stop them being together if that was what they wanted. What Luke wanted, she corrected herself. She knew what she wanted, but what if he didn't feel the same? What if her mother was right? What if he dropped her like a stone now that he'd had what he wanted? She shook her head; no, that wasn't him. At least, she hoped it wasn't him.

But what if her mother had been right about the other stuff, about not having what it took to please a man? Again, she shook her head, this time with a shy smile. There had been no faking his response to her body, to her caresses, just as there had been no faking hers. No, she was worrying over nothing. He'd asked to see her again tonight, hadn't he?

Finishing her toast, she carried her plate and mug to the sink, and was about to head upstairs to shower when she heard the tell-tale crunch of someone walking on her gravelled drive. She frowned in surprise, wondering who would be coming to see her at this hour of the morning, and nearly jumped out of her skin when she saw Luke appear at the back door.

"Luke! You scared me." She placed a hand on her thudding chest.

"I thought I'd call in on my way into work…see if you were up." His smile sent a thrill running through her as he walked into the kitchen and caught her in his arms.

"I also thought maybe you would be worried that I'd got what I came for and you wouldn't see me for dust," he said softly, giving a resigned smile at the telling blush stealing along her cheeks. He shook his head slightly. "You're going to have to trust me."

"I know." She nodded her head. "I'm working on it."

"Good." He released her with a swift kiss before leaning back on the work surface, folding his arms across his chest. "Did you sleep well?"

"I did, thank you." She returned his smile. "Did you?"

"No, I bloody didn't," he complained, his leisurely gaze taking in the tousled curls tumbling down to the small of her back, and the long legs barely covered by her short nightshirt. "I couldn't stop thinking about you."

"Oh!" Chloe gasped, the blush deepening and spreading to her throat.

He moved towards her slowly, desire darkening his eyes, and she felt her breath quicken. When he drew close, she placed her hands on his chest, feeling his heart pounding through the crisp white shirt as he gripped her waist and pulled her against him. He dropped his head to kiss her with a surprising gentleness, and Chloe reached up to bury her fingers in his hair, impatient for a deeper kiss. His response was immediate, his hands moving from her waist to her behind, lifting her up so she could wrap her legs around him.

"God, I want you."

"Well, you'd better let me down." She caught her breath. "You'll never carry me upstairs like this."

"We're not going upstairs," he murmured against her throat, carrying her the short distance to the work surface.

"What? In the kitchen?"

He gave a soft laugh, his lips burning the sensitive hollows of her throat.

"Yes, here in the kitchen."

"But…but that only happens in the movies."

His hands slipped beneath her nightshirt and, as his mouth moved from her throat to her collarbone and then lower, he left her in no further doubt that making love in the kitchen was not simply reserved for Hollywood starlets.

****

Whitby old town was deserted and shrouded in an early morning sea fret, lending a somewhat eerie atmosphere as Chloe walked the short distance from the public car park to the shop she now called work. Pulling the lapels of her coat close around her neck, she could easily imagine Count Dracula stalking one of his hapless victims along this narrow, cobbled street, his cloak flowing out behind him as he swept along. She loved her solitary walk to the shop every morning; just an hour later, and these narrow walkways would be teeming with tourists, despite the approach of autumn. But at this hour, the streets of Whitby were filled with a magical timelessness.

Arriving at the shop and about to put her key in the lock, she noticed the lights were already on inside, and she pushed open the door in surprise.

"Morning." Mark Cameron was bending over the counter with a magnifying glass, studying one of his photographs in closer detail. He looked up as she walked in. "It's a chilly one today."

"It is indeed." She shrugged out of her jacket and walked through to hang it up in the corridor at the back of the shop. "What are you doing in so early?"

"Charming." He smiled when she came to stand beside him at the counter, and pointed to a mug of black coffee. "And here I am, all organised with a coffee for you."

"Thank you." She sipped gingerly from the mug, found it wasn't too hot, and took a large swallow. Although they were still getting to know each other, Mark was easy to work for. Similar in age to her, he was tall and thin, with an outdoorsy style that suited him well. She raised her eyebrows. "And you know what I meant. You said you were going to be out all day on a shoot."

"I am," he admitted. "Just needed to check out a couple of things before I go." He straightened up to favour her with a keen glance. "So, how are you finding it? You've settled in pretty well, from my point of view. And your jewellery seems to be selling well. Any regrets?"

"Oh no, I'm loving it, I really am." She put down her mug and swept her arms wide as if to encompass the entire shop. "It's so lovely speaking to so many different people when they come in, and talking to them about the photographs you take. It doesn't really feel like work." She suddenly paused, biting her lip. "Not that I don't take it seriously. I do. I make sure I keep on top of the online sales and everything, and the books here—"

"Enough, enough." He held up his hand to stop her. "I know you take it seriously; my business has never been in better hands administratively. Dad played a blinder when he suggested you come and work here with me, and I'm extremely grateful to him."

Alone in the shop once Mark had gone off on his shoot, Chloe perched on the stool behind the counter, listening to the soft sounds of the ambient music coming through the speakers, and pulled the stock list towards her. But instead of looking through the papers, she glanced across to where her jewellery display stood in the far corner window, and couldn't help the little shiver of happiness that tingled along her spine.

It was real; she was really selling her own jewellery in a proper shop. The silver rings and earrings were displayed among carefully placed pieces of driftwood and shells. While Mark had congratulated her on her sales, she knew it was still early days. Hopefully, her sales would steadily increase, particularly in the height of the tourist season. There were no regrets, certainly; only perhaps a little wistfulness at not seeing Luke every day.

She reached down to the shelf underneath the counter, and drew out a little tea caddy. On her first morning at the shop—after Mark had given her a tour of the building and talked her through her main duties—he had pointed to a small brown box sitting on the countertop, telling her it had been delivered early that morning.

Chloe's name had been scrawled in capital letters across the top. It wasn't particularly heavy and, upon opening it, she had given a gasp of surprise. Nestled inside, on a bed of crumpled white tissue paper, was an exquisite, hand-painted tea caddy. The oval-shaped tin box was small enough to sit on the palm of her hand,

and was beautifully painted with seascapes on each side. Clearly an antique, it was in excellent condition, and Chloe was utterly captivated.

The hinged lid was topped with a small loop handle, and she had opened it to find a white paper bag inside. Mark had gone into the back to make a coffee, and she had given a small, delighted laugh when she opened the bag to find it contained Edinburgh rock. Luke. He must have seen the collection of antique tea caddies sitting on a high shelf in her kitchen. Carefully setting the little caddy on the counter, she picked up the box once more and found a small card tucked down the side of the tissue paper.

Saw this and thought of you. Good luck on your first day. L xx

Filled with a warm glow whenever she looked at it, Chloe opened it now and took out a piece of rock before carefully stowing it back on the shelf.

The morning passed quickly with a steady stream of customers, and she was just thinking longingly of the sandwich waiting for her in the fridge, when the couple who had been staring at a large, framed photograph of the Abbey caught her eye.

"Can I help you?"

"Yes. We can't make up our mind about this one." The man frowned at the picture but fell silent.

"It's beautiful, isn't it?" Chloe prompted.

"It is." Once again, he and his wife simply stared at the photograph.

"You're hesitating," she said with a smile. She was vaguely aware of the doorbell indicating another customer had entered the shop, but wanted to make sure she helped this couple with whatever it was they needed.

"It's just…it's rather large." His wife rubbed her chin thoughtfully. "We were thinking it would go in the dining room, but we're not sure if it would just overpower everything."

Chloe nodded in understanding. "Well, I guess it depends on whether you think the room is big enough to take it. What's the décor like? If your room is fairly plain and minimalistic, then this would look stunning, a real centrepiece. But if your style is less minimal, with large print wallpaper or strong furnishings, there's a risk it might feel as if the picture is competing with everything else for attention."

"Hmm, yes, I see your point." The man looked at his wife and grinned. "I wouldn't say our style is particularly minimalistic."

"But I really love this picture." The woman appeared torn.

"Well, if it's the viewpoint and the setting you like, we have two smaller photographs of the Abbey, taken from the same point, but in contrasting light—so one during the day, and one during the night. They're quite beautiful together, actually."

Chloe took the couple to the other side of the room where the two photographs were set side by side.

"Oh, now they're just lovely."

"Or, if you feel these two are still a little on the large side, we have four smaller prints, again with the same setting, but this time showing the Abbey in each of the four seasons."

Again, she showed them the framed photographs, and smiled at the indecision clouding their faces. "Have I just made it even more difficult?"

"They're all so beautiful. We just love this view of the Abbey, and wanted to buy a really nice photograph."

"Well, see which you think would fit best in your dining room, bearing in mind the size of the space you want to fill, and the décor around it. The frames they've currently got are quite neutral, but if you wanted a particular style or colour, we have quite a good range I can show you. Just let me know."

About to leave them alone to consider, she paused when the woman nodded decisively. "No. We'll take the four seasonal photographs. I can picture them in the dining room perfectly."

"Fabulous." Chloe took the framed photographs to the counter, glancing around the shop as she did so. Her stomach did a little flip when she realised it was Luke who had come into the shop, and was now slowly walking around and viewing the photographs. Returning her attention to her two customers, she carefully wrapped the framed prints and was ringing them through the till when the woman handed Chloe a pair of earrings from her display.

"Can I take these as well, please?"

"Of course." She placed the earrings in a small jewellery box. "Did you want them in the same bag?"

"Oh no, I don't want to risk losing them. I'll pop them in my handbag." The woman smiled as she did so. "The gentleman over there said you made these yourself. You're very clever. They're beautiful."

"Oh, thank you." She blushed as she handled the card transaction and gave the customers their framed prints and receipts. "Thank you very much, and I hope we'll see you again."

Luke immediately came over to the counter as the two customers left the shop. "Hey, good afternoon."

"Hello."

"You're quite the saleswoman, Miss MacGregor. I was impressed." He glanced around to make sure no-one else was in the shop before leaning across the counter to kiss her. "A woman of many talents."

"Thank you. I'm really enjoying myself."

"I can see that. It's good." He gave a rueful smile. "I'm just passing by, I'm afraid, but I wanted to check we're still on for dinner tonight?"

"Yes, of course." She gave a soft laugh. "You are allowed to walk by and not pop in, you know."

"I know, but I couldn't resist." He dropped another swift kiss on her lips before turning towards the door. "I'll pick you up at seven."

****

The dulcet tones of Andrea Bocelli filled the little cottage as Chloe added the finishing touches to her make-up. She had chosen a simple, navy blue tea dress with tiny white polka dots which she would wear with a pair of matching navy dolly shoes. Hooking a pair of long, over-sized silver earrings into her ears, she paused, straining to hear over the soaring voice of the tenor. She could have sworn she heard a door bang, and was that Jasper barking?

Running lightly down the stairs, she turned towards the living room and came to an abrupt halt.

The front door was open.

Her heart gave a painful, solid thump in her chest and her breath stilled in her throat. She stared at the door. She hadn't left it open, and it was too heavy to have blown open in the wind. Besides, the weather was calm tonight.

She could hear Jasper barking and scratching at a door somewhere in the small cottage, and the hairs on the nape of Chloe's neck lifted.

Something wasn't right.

Her legs felt awkward and stiff as she forced herself to walk slowly towards the living room, taking long deep breaths, and trying to ignore the sense of dread stealing over her. She told herself she was being ridiculous. What on earth was she afraid of?

As she turned into the living room, she saw someone leaning casually on her mantelpiece, and the breath left her body in a rush.

Chris.

Chapter Eleven

"Hello, babe, surprised to see me?"

His voice was barely audible over the opera still blaring out. Chloe reached across to the CD player sitting on a shelf next to the door, and switched it off. She didn't take her eyes from the man standing by the fire. Silence filled the room, broken only by the sound of Jasper barking and scratching at the workroom door.

"Thank Christ for that." Chris favoured her with a derisive smile. "You always did have crap taste in music."

"What are you doing, Chris? How dare you just walk into my house?" She forced herself to meet his gaze without flinching. *Don't let him know you're frightened.*

He grinned. "You look a little surprised. Wondering how I found you?" He picked up one of the shells on her mantelpiece, turning it over in his hands as if examining it, before putting it back. "Oh, I've known where you live for a long time, Chloe. Just been playing a waiting game; waiting for the right moment, you know?"

She stared at him, struggling to maintain a calm expression as he confirmed her worst fears. She'd been a fool to think he would just give up, that she could carry on as if he'd never existed.

"And now the stars have aligned." He gestured towards the heavens with a mocking grin. "No injunction, and no Hardaker's to hide behind. I could almost believe you were deliberately making it easy for me."

"So, you just decided to walk into my house uninvited?" She spoke with a bravery she didn't feel.

"Hey, what can I say? I knocked." He gave a shrug. "Not my fault if you couldn't hear me over all that bloody caterwauling."

Jasper gave a loud yelp behind the door to her right, but when she moved towards it, Chris moved to block her path with a speed that surprised her.

"I think the dog is just fine where it is."

"What do you want?"

"I just thought I'd call in and see how you are." He dropped his head on one side, spreading his hands wide as if surprised by her lack of enthusiasm.

"Well, as you can see, I'm fine so you can go now." Again, she lifted her chin in a defiant gesture, determined not to show any weakness.

"Babe, I'm hurt. I thought we could catch up, talk about old times." He held up a hand to stall her next words. "And I've got something I think you might be interested in."

"I can't think of anything you have that I would be interested in." She deliberately looked at her watch. "Look, whatever it is, make it quick, will you?"

"Make it quick?" He dropped his voice suggestively. "Now that sounds like an invitation."

He moved towards her, slowly and deliberately, and despite her defiance, she could feel her legs begin to tremble, could feel herself struggling to breath.

"Don't you come near me, Chris. Not one more step."

To her relief, he paused, but his amused grin did little to reassure her. "I like this new, brave Chloe. Kind of turns me on."

"I mean it. Don't you touch me." She reached out to her right, her thumping heart missing a beat when her fingers closed around a heavy, glass paperweight. She held it up, biting her lip when she saw how much her hand was shaking. A quick glance towards Chris confirmed he had also noticed, and he gave a mocking laugh.

"Brave words." His voice was goading now. "But you haven't got the guts."

"Try me." Her voice wavered slightly as he continued to move slowly towards her, and she gave one last attempt at warning him off. "You'd better leave. Luke will be here any minute."

Chris stopped, his expression darkening. "That would be Mr. High and Mighty Luke Warwick, would it?" He moved suddenly to close the gap between them, as if tiring of the game. "What's he got that I haven't?"

A cold anger settled over her; anger at once again finding herself at the mercy of a man, and shame at her attempt to use Luke as a shield to prevent whatever it was Chris was intending to do. She took a step towards him, raising the paperweight to shoulder height and leaning forwards until her face was just inches from his.

"Back. Off."

Surprise and awareness flickered over his face and, after a moment, he stepped back and shoved his hands in his jacket pocket, shifting his shoulders uncomfortably. "Christ, you've lost your sense of humour."

His eyes suddenly widened as if remembering what it was he came for, and he looked down at his pocket, withdrawing what looked like a CD. His earlier cocky attitude returned, and he wandered over to settle himself on her sofa.

"You know, seeing you at that charity night got me to thinking," he said, conversationally. "I couldn't work out what this Warwick guy was getting out of seeing you. Knowing, as I do, your…performance issues, shall we say."

"So, you've come all this way to insult me?" Her mouth twisted in derision. "I don't think you can better the insults you threw at me that night, Chris, so why don't you leave?"

"No, no, you've got me all wrong," he said, arranging his features into a hurt expression. "No, it's not that at all. I came over to congratulate you."

Chloe didn't respond, unsure where he was going with this line of conversation.

"It all became clear this week, and I must say, I'm thrilled to see you took my advice." His eyes sparkled maliciously as he watched for her response. When she remained silent, his smile broadened. "You know, the advice about getting some lessons. I'm assuming you've come to some sort of arrangement with Warwick. You get a bit of practice, learn a few things about what a man needs in the bedroom, and in turn, he's able to satisfy those natural urges that would otherwise go unmet…you know, given his wife's current condition. I guess it's a win-win situation."

A shiver of unease traced along her spine. "I don't know what you're talking about, but I want you to leave now. Before I call the police."

"You do know about his wife, don't you?" His gaze searched her face as if wanting to capture any hint of distress, savouring her discomfort before continuing. "Oh, this is priceless. I was obviously crediting you with too much intelligence, but I should have known better. You're so bloody naive."

"Luke isn't married. You're lying."

"You mean he hasn't told you?" Chris feigned surprise. "I guess it must have slipped his mind. Well, surely, he's told you he's about to become a father?"

"Get out." She whispered, closing her eyes as her head began to whirl. "Just go."

"I didn't think he'd told you; he hasn't the guts, and you always were gullible," he sneered derisively, and seeing the confusion and hurt in her eyes, began to laugh. "Oh, poor Chloe. Did you really think he cared about you? Could you possibly have been that deluded?"

He waved the disc he had taken from his pocket, and she realised it wasn't a CD after all; it was a DVD. "I figured you wouldn't take my word for it, so I've brought proof. I think you'll find it interesting."

She wanted to tell him to stop, that she wasn't interested in whatever was on the disc, but the words stuck in her throat. She just stood there and watched as he moved towards the television and DVD player as if he owned the place, deftly inserting the disc and grasping the remote controls to press play. As the screen flickered into life, he pressed fast forward and lazily watched the fleeting images, speaking to Chloe over his shoulder as he did so.

"You've actually got Lisa to thank for putting you

out of your deluded naivety. She's been annoying the crap out of me, banging on about us getting married, bringing home bloody wedding brochures and leaflets. Anyway, some randomer at her work brought in a wedding video to show her the venue and, I'll give her her due, eagle-eyed Lisa spotted someone familiar on the video. Brought it home to show me. Gotta say, it really made my night when I recognised old Warwick there on the video. I just love this whole six degrees of separation thing, don't you?" He chattered on aimlessly, his eyes glittering spitefully as she stared at the screen, unable to look away. "Ah, here we go."

The video panned slowly across the beautifully manicured grounds of a large country house, pausing briefly on individual guests before moving on. She gasped when it stopped at a couple in the foreground; Luke was instantly recognisable, and holding lightly on to his arm, was an attractive, heavily pregnant woman. The couple were unaware of the camera focussed on them and, as Chloe watched in fascinated horror, she saw the woman suddenly take Luke's hand and hold it against her swollen stomach. His face broke into a delighted grin when he obviously felt the baby kicking against his hand, and he embraced the woman tightly.

Chloe swayed as a wave of dizziness swept over her, the paperweight falling onto the cushions as she gripped the back of the sofa, unable to tear her gaze from the screen. Off camera, someone could be heard calling for Mrs. Warwick, and both Luke and the woman turned towards the unseen speaker, the woman answering "Yes?" and leaving Chloe in no doubt whatsoever that she was, indeed, Luke's wife.

"When was this?" Her voice cracked, and she

pressed her hand to her mouth, fighting against nausea.

"Dunno, a month, six weeks ago—" His eyes widened in surprise, and he shot to his feet, his gaze fixed on something behind her.

Confused and disorientated, she turned to see Luke standing in the doorway, having obviously found the front door open. From the look of horror and disbelief on his face, it was obvious he'd seen the DVD.

"Chloe—"

"No!" She didn't want to see him, talk to him, listen to him. She didn't want anything to do with him. Blinking away the tears blurring her vision, she slapped away his outstretched hand, and pushed past him to flee through the door and out into the night.

****

Luke stood in the doorway, feeling as if he was in some sort of nightmare, vaguely aware of Jasper barking and scratching behind the door on the opposite side of the room. About to go and let her out, his gaze swung to where Chris was hurriedly ejecting the DVD. White hot anger flooded through him, and he crossed the room with a speed which shocked the other man.

"You bastard." Almost without realising what he was doing, Luke grabbed him, and shoved him against the wall, his forearm under Chris's chin. He shook with the effort it took to retain some semblance of self-control.

"Do you have any idea what you've done?" His voice was low and clipped. "Haven't you hurt her enough?"

"I was letting her know the truth." Chris clutched ineffectually at Luke's arm, managing a smug smile despite the pressure against his windpipe. "You're the one hurting her now."

Luke closed his eyes and took a deep breath. This man had systematically abused her, both verbally and physically. God, he wanted to kill him. He opened his eyes and looked into Chris's face, saw the man's eyes widen in sudden fear when he recognised the intent in his gaze.

He could do it, too; one less bastard in the world.

But then he thought of Chloe, of his grandfather, of their sense of what was right and wrong, and he reluctantly relaxed his grip.

"If I ever see you again, if you ever come within a mile of Chloe, I'll kill you."

Luke dragged him from the cottage and thrust him towards the car parked on the drive. He watched as the terrified man fumbled with his car keys before getting in and driving off with a squeal of rubber on tarmac.

Luke immediately made for the cliff path, knowing Chloe would have instinctively headed for the beach. The evening light was fading and, as he ran down the path, his gaze scanned the beach, grimacing when he saw the tide was almost in.

And then he saw her, wading out into the sea.

He skidded to a halt.

"Chloe, no," he breathed. It was nothing more than a whisper, but it set him into action, and he flung himself down the rest of the path, somehow keeping his footing until he reached the sand below.

Racing across the narrow stretch of beach not yet submerged by the incoming tide, he called her name repeatedly, but she was either choosing to ignore him or simply didn't hear him, because she gave no response whatsoever. She had stopped moving now and was simply standing thigh-deep in the mercifully calm ocean, staring out towards the horizon.

"Chloe!" He waded towards her, and was reaching for her hand when she turned to him. The tracks of her tears shone silver across her face in the fading light. They stared at each other in silence, and then—

"You...you—" She was barely able to spit the words out. "After everything I said, everything you said."

Taking him by surprise, she suddenly shoved at his chest and, caught off balance, he fell backwards into the ocean. He floundered in the water for a moment until he managed to force his feet down onto the shifting sands. Orienting himself, he saw she had almost made it back to the shore, and he waded after her.

She had only managed a couple of steps onto the sand before he reached her and caught her arm, swinging her around to face him.

"Chloe, wait. Just listen to me." He shook his head, brushing a hand over his face impatiently to try and clear the salt water from his eyes.

"Listen? You want me to listen?" She slapped his hands away. "How very convenient for you to forget you had a wife and baby on the way. Just when were you thinking of telling me, Luke? Maybe ring me from the delivery room, or were you going to wait and send me an invitation to the christening?"

"Don't be ridiculous." He thrust a hand through his dripping hair before taking a steadying breath. "Look, if you'll let me explain, I—"

"No, I won't," she cut him off, stumbling backwards in the stand. "I won't listen to any more of your lies. My God, no wonder you weren't able to offer me a commitment! What about all the stuff you told me about your grandfather? Was that all lies, too? I really hope so because, if not, he must be turning in his grave."

Without waiting for a response, she spun away from him. Cursing under his breath, he moved quickly to catch her hand, forcing her to stop.

"So that's it? You're not going to give me a chance to explain?"

"No." She snatched her hand from his, her face crumpling as she covered her ears, fingers curled into fists, shaking her head desperately. "No, I'm not. Because you'll make me believe you. You'll make it all sound so logical, so ridiculously simple, and how could I have been so stupid? But it will all be lies. Everything about you is a lie. So, no I won't listen to you anymore."

Luke stared at her in disbelief and disappointment. *Did she really have so little faith in him? So little trust?*

The tide swirled around his ankles, taking him by surprise. A quick glance told him they were in danger of being cut off, and he swore softly. He caught hold of her wrist, pulling her with him as he strode towards the cliff path.

"We need to get off this beach."

Chloe dug her heels in, pulling against him ineffectually.

"Are *you* going to drag me around, too? Knock some sense into me?"

He drew in a sharp breath and spun around to face her, snatching his hand back as if her skin burned his fingers, shocked to the core by her words.

"Chloe?" His voice broke as he stared at her,

willing her to retract the words.

You didn't mean that. Tell me you didn't mean that.

Her eyes were wide above the hands that covered her mouth, as if to prevent any further accusations, and she backed away from him shaking her head. A moment later, she turned and ran across the quickly diminishing strip of sand towards the cliff path.

Luke made no attempt to follow her and just stood there, his world crumbling around him as he struggled to breathe. He felt numb, unable to move, unable to feel.

Without warning his legs gave way, and he dropped to his knees on the wet sand, pressing the heels of his hands into his eyes to stem the tears, and a strangled sob tore through him. He'd been so terrified of hurting her, but now the reality hit home.

From the very first moment he had been drawn to her, he had been convinced his reluctance to get involved had been borne out of a fear of hurting her. What he hadn't understood until now was that his fear had also been borne of the knowledge that she had the power to hurt him, too.

****

Chloe ran across the garden, almost blinded by tears, and shot into the cottage. She slammed the door closed and pushed the locks home, before leaning back against it and sinking to the floor. But the sound of Jasper still barking and scratching from inside her workroom forced her back to her feet, and she freed the dog, pushing Jasper down when she leaped up at her immediately, whining in distress and relief at finally being set free. Numb with shock, and shivering from reaction and cold, she climbed the stairs and stripped off the wet dress before crawling into bed. Curled up in a ball and sobbing into her pillow, she cursed herself for ever believing that things might be different this time.

Stupid, stupid, stupid.

Gullible, naïve, pretty packaging, not ready for commitment—why didn't she ever learn?

Luke had told her over and over that he was not looking for a long-term relationship, that he didn't want to get involved, and yet his actions had not reflected those words. He had shown her tenderness, had been so protective, had made her believe he cared despite his words.

And she had believed him.

Her thoughts drifted back to that morning after the storm, when he'd said she must never have truly been in love. She remembered how she had told him she didn't believe in love.

What a fool she'd been, even convincing herself that she didn't want anything more from him. And without realising it, she had gone ahead and fallen in love with this man, fallen in love with his goodness, his sense of duty, and his desperate need to do the right thing. How ironic that the man she had fallen in love with didn't actually exist, had been a sham. Once again, she had allowed herself to hope that her mother was wrong, that she deserved to find happiness.

She eventually drifted into a fitful sleep, only to awaken during the early hours to sit bolt upright, joy flooding through her. What if the woman in the video was his sister? But, as she blinked away the cobwebs of sleep, her happiness melted away. No, that couldn't be right. If she were his sister, she wouldn't have been called *Mrs*. Warwick. Besides, they had not acted like siblings. Sinking back onto her pillow, sleep remained elusive, and she tossed and turned until the chill light of dawn filtered through her curtains.

She stared up at the ceiling, her eyes feeling as if they were full of sand, and listened to Jasper snoring softly in her basket by the door. He would come around to the cottage to explain, she knew he would. He would try and convince her of his innocence, tell her she'd got it all wrong.

She closed her eyes, choking back a sob, wincing as burning tears slipped from beneath her lids and rolled down into her hair. She couldn't be here when he did, she couldn't allow him to convince her once again.

That thought gave her the strength to climb out of bed and stumble into the shower. Half an hour later, she locked the cottage door, shoved her overnight bag in the boot of her car, and opened Jasper's travel cage. The dog leapt in happily, excited to be going on an adventure, and Chloe managed a listless smile. Oh, to be as carefree as her dog. Fighting the urge to glance across the headland to Luke's cottage, she climbed into her car and started the engine.

****

It was still dark outside, but the first rays of the morning sun were beginning to peep over the horizon. Luke was sitting at the kitchen table, his hands cupped around an untouched mug of coffee that had long since grown cold, but he made no move to refresh it. He closed his eyes as a vision of Chloe's distraught face floated into his thoughts, and he shook his head to drive the image from his mind. Pushing himself away from the table, he paced the kitchen, unable to shake the uncomfortable feeling of helplessness engulfing him. Her words about his grandfather turning in his grave, the suggestion that he might hit her, burned in his stomach, and he strode across to the front door, shrugging on a fleece and walking out across the cliff top as if he could outpace those awful accusations. He deliberately turned away from the path leading down to the beach.

He had tried so hard to stay away from her, but it had proved simply impossible for him, not least because it had been complicated by the fact that they had to work together. But if he were being honest with himself, he knew he wouldn't have been able to stay away from her even if she hadn't worked for him. There was something about her that he was drawn to, something that pulled him to her against his will.

He gave a humourless laugh as he remembered those conversations where he had told her about not being ready for commitment; that he would fall in love when he was ready. God, how naïve he had been to believe he could choose when to fall in love and when not to. He had fallen in love with her without even realising it, against his better judgement. His entire purpose had been to avoid hurting her and, through no fault of his own, he'd ended up hurting her anyway.

He was lost, had no idea where to go or what to do next. For the first time in his life, he was frightened. Frightened that he had fallen in love; frightened that he had truly hurt someone; and frightened that the person he had fallen in love with was the wrong person.

Once again, he heard those awful, gut-wrenching, wailing sobs coming from his mother's bedroom as his twelve-year-old self buried his head in a pillow, trying to drown out the sounds of her despair.

Two hours later he found himself at Chloe's door. Although it was still early, he had no doubt she would have had an equally restless night and would more than likely be up already. He hesitated for a moment, suddenly overtaken by the feeling he was too late, and took a step back to look up at the first-floor windows. All the curtains were open, including those hanging in Chloe's bedroom; he'd been right, she was already awake. He knocked on the door and waited, listening intently. He could hear no sounds of movement from within and, with little expectation, raised his hand to rap on the door loudly once more.

Ordinarily, Jasper would have been barking and scrabbling at the door by now, but there was nothing but silence, aside from the gentle tinkling of shells stirring in the breeze in the garden behind him. He moved around to peer in the living room window and then around the back to knock on the kitchen door.

He knew now without a doubt that she wasn't in. Unless the weather was particularly bad, the kitchen door was always open to allow Jasper to run in and out as she pleased. That heavy feeling of helplessness settled over him once more as he crossed to the garage and looked through the window to find it empty.

He turned around slowly, surveying the cottage and her garden; it seemed empty and lifeless, proof if it were needed that she was gone.

His lips tightened when he pulled out his mobile phone and saw the slight tremor in his fingers when he punched in her number, waiting for it to connect. It tripped straight to voicemail and he closed his eyes, fighting against a feeling of despair.

"Chloe, I need to talk to you. Please call me back as soon as you get this message. It's important."

His gaze settled on the garden swing at the very bottom of her garden, and he made his way down the path to sit and wait for her return, shivering as the cool morning air stole through his fleece. He sat as if in a daze, lost in thought and memories until he became aware that the sun had risen high in the sky and he was beginning to feel uncomfortably warm. Glancing at his watch, he was surprised to realise it was lunchtime; clearly Chloe was not coming home. He tried to call her again, but this time it didn't even trip through to voicemail. This time a disembodied voice simply told him his call couldn't be connected.

She had blocked his number.

Chapter Twelve

Claire MacGregor was cutting fresh roses from the neat row of bushes in her front garden when Chloe pulled her car onto the drive. She looked up in surprise and gave a puzzled but welcoming smile as her daughter walked around to the boot and pulled out her overnight bag, reaching across to open Jasper's cage.

"Chloe, darling, I wasn't expecting you today."

Having maintained her composure on the drive over to her mother's, Chloe couldn't hold back the tears any longer and she began to sob. Claire immediately dropped the cut roses onto the grass and hurried over to her daughter.

"Darling, whatever is the matter?"

Hiccupping against her tears, she shook her head. "Oh Mum. I've been so stupid."

With a knowing glance, Claire moved to embrace her, pulling her into her arms and holding her tight.

"It's all right, darling. It's all right," she said softly. "You're home now."

****

Curled up on the familiar sofa with a steaming cup of coffee and a plate of buttered toast, Chloe favoured her mother with a wary glance. "Please don't say I told you so."

"As if I would." Claire gave her a reproachful

glance, but was unable to resist adding a further comment. "Besides, I don't need to; you already knew it was bound to happen."

Chloe gave a weary sigh, untucking her legs from the sofa and setting down her mug. "I knew coming here was a bad idea. I don't know why I expected anything different…"

"Oh Chloe, I'm sorry," said Claire, quickly. "Please don't go. This is your home, of course this is where you should be when you've been hurt."

Chloe looked uncertain when her mother moved to sit next to her on the sofa, reaching out to take hold of her hand. "Tell me what happened, love."

After a brief hesitation, she painfully recalled all that had happened from the time she first met Luke, up to the awful realisation last night that he was married. Claire listened in silence, gripping Chloe's hand tightly.

"How could all this happen to you, without you telling me?" For the first time Chloe could ever remember, awareness sharpened her mother's gaze. "Are we really so far apart? Am I so awful a mother that you can't talk to me?"

Chloe stared at her hand clasped in her mother's but didn't respond. *What could she say?*

There was a long silence as Claire acknowledged her daughter's silence until, eventually, she squeezed Chloe's hand and swallowed hard.

"Well, you're here now, darling. And you can stay as long as you need to."

Obviously deciding to give her some space, Claire busied herself around the house, leaving Chloe to her thoughts. For her part, Chloe remained curled up on the sofa, replaying every conversation she had ever had with Luke, every kiss, every touch. Despite his betrayal, she yearned for him. She also burned with guilt. What she had said to him about knocking some sense into her; that had been awful, and the memory of his agonized expression haunted her. She hadn't meant it; she knew without doubt that he would never lift a finger to her. But she had wanted to hurt him, as he had hurt her.

Her mobile phone vibrated on the sofa next to her, reminding her that she had a voicemail message. She stared at the phone, knowing it would be from him. Part of her desperately wanted to hear his voice, but after a brief hesitation, she deleted the message without listening to it.

At that moment, her mother breezed in with a vase full of the cut roses and placed them on the hearth in front of the empty fireplace, before turning an appraising glance on her daughter. For a moment, she looked as if she might speak, but in the end, she simply smiled and went back to the kitchen.

A humourless smile touched Chloe's lips. She was quite impressed by her mother's unusual restraint. She knew Claire would be dying to launch into her usual criticism and disparagement of the male population, could see the satisfaction in her mother's face as she nodded to herself, obviously pleased to find she had been proved right...again.

She closed her eyes. She wasn't sure how long she would be able to manage staying at her mother's house. Much as she loved her, Claire was hard work and her constant negativity towards any man was depressing.

As it turned out, Claire managed to hold her tongue until early evening when, as they were loading the dishwasher together, she turned to her daughter.

"Oh, darling, it's so lovely having you here. I know you're terribly upset, but believe me, it's for the best." She patted Chloe's cheek gently. "It's better you found out now than later down the line."

Chloe concentrated on breathing steadily, carefully putting away the clean pots and wiping down the worktop.

"I always knew it wouldn't end with that...whatever his name was...Chris. I knew you wouldn't learn." She carried on, oblivious to Chloe's stricken face. "You always were stubborn, refusing to listen to a word I said, despite the traumatic experience I went through. No. I knew you would carry on, pretending everything would be all right. This had to happen, darling. This was the only way you were going to learn."

"Mum!" Chloe finally snapped, but quickly reigned in her temper. She took a deep breath, and forced herself to continue in a calmer voice. "I'm tired and it's been a long day. If it's okay with you, I think I'll go for a bath and head off to bed."

"Oh." Claire looked surprised and a little disappointed, but recovered swiftly. "Of course, darling. You get a good night's sleep, and everything will seem much better in the morning."

Pouring a lavender scented oil into the bath and swirling the hot water around with her fingers, Chloe wished she shared her mother's optimism. Right now, it was difficult to believe anything would ever seem all right ever again.

****

Luke drew the car to a halt at the kerbside to

consult the street map he had printed off last night. Chloe had mentioned the village where her mother lived, but he didn't know the address, and he had decided to drive around in the hope of seeing her car. That was always assuming she was at her mother's house, of course. It was equally likely that she had gone to stay with her friend, Sean and his wife, but he had no idea where they lived, and he was simply unable to sit at home. Not being able to do anything was driving him crazy.

He blew out a long, frustrated sigh as he crossed off yet another street on his map. It was like looking for a needle in a haystack, but what else could he do? With no better idea forthcoming, he tossed the paper onto the passenger seat, put the car in gear, and resumed his circuit of the village.

The early morning sun shone directly into his eyes as he turned into the next street, and he flicked the visor down in irritation. It would be just his luck to get pulled over for kerb crawling. He smiled without humour, but the next minute his breath caught in his throat.

There was her car, parked on the driveway of a semi-detached house a little further along the street. He checked and double checked the license plate; it was hers.

Reversing a little way down the street, he pulled over onto the opposite side, his heart beating frantically in his chest, and switched off the engine. Now he was here, his resolved faltered; her final words rang in his ears and he shook his head as if to deny them.

He gave an irritated sigh. Now that he'd found her, was he really going to just sit here? With a muttered curse, he leaned across to check his appearance in the rear-view mirror, and winced. Not his finest hour. Stubble darkened his chin, and the lines around his eyes hinted at a lack of sleep. Well, there was nothing he could do about that now.

As he walked up the quiet, well-kept residential street, he wondered how on earth he was going to persuade Chloe to hear him out. And that was supposing she would even see him. He was still stunned by the thought that she believed he could ever hurt her.

Claire MacGregor's garden was immaculate, with a carefully manicured, small square of lawn bordered by closely planted rose bushes. It was a far cry from her daughter's eclectic garden full of mismatched flowers, bushes, and seashells. Taking a deep breath, he pressed the doorbell and stood back.

He didn't have to wait for long. The door was opened by an attractive woman in her mid-forties, her blonde bob framing a smooth face, with carefully applied make-up despite the relatively early hour on this Sunday morning. She wore a pair of dark blue jeans that emphasised her slim figure, with a white blouse and navy-blue silk scarf. She looked expectantly at the stranger standing on her doorstep, and gave him a brief, impersonal smile.

"Mrs. MacGregor?" he said quietly. "I'd like to see Chloe, if I may?"

The change in her demeanour was immediate. The smile vanished and her dark blue eyes grew even darker. "It's you, isn't it?" Her voice dripped ice. "I can't believe you have the gall to stand there asking to see my daughter. Well, she doesn't want to see you. You have had a wasted journey. Please leave."

She began to close the door, and looked up in

surprise when his hand shot out to hold it open.

"Please, can you tell her I'm here?" He kept his voice quiet and even, but determined.

"I've told you, she doesn't want to see you," Claire snapped, leaning forward to sneer at him. "You men are all the same; only after one thing. Well, you got what you wanted, now you can just go."

"If I was only after one thing, why would I be here now?" He couldn't help being drawn into responding to her generalisation, and took a deep breath. "Mrs. MacGregor, please, I need to speak to her."

"She's not here."

He gave an impatient sigh. "Look, I know she's here, her car is on the drive."

"I mean she's not here now, she's gone for a walk, trying to clear her head." She tried unsuccessfully to close the door, but he continued to hold it open. "Please let go of my door or I shall have no alternative but to call the police."

"Mrs. MacGregor—"

"Chloe is trying to rebuild her life once again, and I would appreciate it if you would allow her to do so." She looked him up and down. "I can't imagine why you insisted on coming over here to see her. It is patently obvious she is never going to be able to keep a man. You'd be better off saving your efforts and either concentrating on your wife, or moving to the next woman on your list."

"Would you just listen to yourself?" He could hear his voice rising, and checked himself. "There's little wonder Chloe doesn't trust me, or any man. You've filled her head with all this crap about her not being good enough. Do you have any idea what you've done to your own daughter?"

"How dare you?" Claire blanched at his accusation, but retained enough awareness to glance past him to make sure there was no one else around.

"I can dare a little louder, if you really want to give the neighbours something to talk about." He gave a humourless smile when she once again checked the street outside. "Unless you want me to cause a scene, I suggest you let me in to wait for Chloe."

After a moment's hesitation, she reluctantly stepped aside to allow him into the living room. Quivering with rage, she stalked into the room and rounded on him.

"How dare you presume to talk to me about my daughter," she hissed. "You have no idea what you are talking about, what we've been through—"

"Chloe told me about her father," he cut in sharply. "And while I am deeply sympathetic for the way he treated you, it in no way excuses what you have done, and are still doing, to her."

Claire opened her mouth to retaliate, but he carried on without pausing. "You have convinced your daughter that she is worthless, did you know that? She believes she is worthless, that she has nothing to offer in a relationship." He stared at her in distaste. "How can you possibly sleep at night?"

"I…I…" She struggled in the face of his accusations. "I have done my best to protect her from men like you. I have never done anything except to try and protect her, while you on the other hand—"

"I love her," he interrupted, smiling grimly when she gasped and stopped mid-sentence. "I love her and, given the chance, I believe she could love me, too. Can you somehow not see how much love she has to give? Don't you want her to be happy, to have children of her own? Or are you so selfish as to want her to grow old alone?"

Claire was saved the need to respond by the sound of the front door opening and, seconds later, Jasper ran into the room, giving a delighted bark when she recognised Luke standing in front of the fireplace. Chloe followed close behind, but halted in the doorway, her eyes widening in surprise and dismay.

The atmosphere in the room was charged as they stared at each other in silence, both acknowledging the visible evidence of a sleepless night.

"Chloe..." Claire fell silent as Luke strode across the room.

He automatically reached for her hand, but froze in sudden memory of her last words to him and instead let it drop to his side.

"We need to talk. Will you come with me?"

She closed her eyes briefly in recognition of his hesitation, but when she began to shake her head, he held out his hand again. "If you want me to leave, I will. Of course, I will. But, Chloe, please at least just let me talk to you."

For the longest moment, he thought she was going to refuse, but then she gave a brief nod. "Okay."

He gestured towards the door, indicating she should go first, careful to keep his distance when she walked out in silence.

"I'll bring her back later." He only just managed to keep his voice civil as he left Claire in the living room.

They walked in silence to his car and, as Chloe got in the passenger side, he walked around and got in the driver's side. Pulling the door closed, she stared through the windscreen with her arms folded across her chest.

"Put your seatbelt on." Luke clicked his own seatbelt in place.

Startled her out of her silence, she turned to him in surprise. "What? I thought you wanted to talk. Where are we going?"

"Put. Your seatbelt. On." He struggled to contain his growing anger. She was treating him as if he were some kind of monster. When had he ever given her any reason to be afraid of him? He turned to look at her, meeting her gaze until she looked away. After a brief hesitation, she pulled on her seatbelt and resumed her position of staring through the windscreen.

Satisfied, he switched on the engine and pulled out onto the road in silence.

****

"Where are we going?" They had been driving for almost an hour, and not a single word had passed between them. When he remained silent, she tried again. "Luke."

"To meet someone," he answered shortly.

"Who?"

His hands gripped the steering wheel. "Sara."

"Sara," she repeated slowly, before comprehension started to dawn. "Oh please…please, Luke, don't tell me she's your wife."

He ignored her and simply carried on driving as if he hadn't heard, but the pulse throbbing in his jaw belied his calm exterior.

"You're taking me to meet your wife? I don't believe this is happening." She leant towards him in agitation. "No. Stop the car. Luke, please stop the car."

He responded with a stony silence, and she took a breath, ready to insist he stop the car but, as her eyes drew over his face, she noticed the dark stubble, the lines of exhaustion around his eyes, and she hesitated. What was going through his head? What could he possibly gain from taking her to meet his wife? Perhaps they had one of those *open relationships* where they were both free to sleep with other people. She closed her eyes in mortification; that was so not her thing.

A lump formed in her throat as she continued to stare at him, at the man she loved so desperately. He looked as unhappy as she felt. It was obvious he was determined to go through with whatever it was he had planned, and so she sank back into her seat, turning her head to stare sightlessly through the passenger window, feeling sick to the stomach.

Several miles later, they pulled up outside a large detached suburban house sitting on the outskirts of Harrogate. Her stomach churned when he got out and walked around to open her door.

"Why are you doing this?" She looked up at him, making no move to get out of the car.

"Because you've given me no choice," he said tightly, holding out his hand.

"Please, don't do this." She choked back a sob with her hand when he crouched down by the car and, after a brief hesitation, took her hands in his.

"I really need you to trust me," he said softly, gripping her fingers painfully tight. "Just this once."

Searching his face, she saw nothing but openness and honesty, the traits she had fallen in love with. As the silence between them lengthened, he sighed and dipped his head, but not before she glimpsed the hurt and vulnerability in those pale green eyes. She frowned, noting again the stubble darkening his jaw, the tiredness around his eyes, and the pallor of his skin; he was suffering, too. Why that should matter to her she didn't know, but somehow it did.

Pulling her hands from his grasp, she reached for her handbag and drew out a tissue to wipe her eyes and blow her nose. Flicking down the sun visor, she took a quick look in the vanity mirror and winced at the pink nose and slightly red-rimmed eyes staring back at her. Not how she would ideally like to be presented to his wife.

"Okay, you win. Let's get it over with," she said quietly. She kept her eyes downcast, her hands clasped tightly in her lap to prevent them from shaking.

Luke leaned into the car and took her face in his hands, hesitating for a split second before kissing her gently. A half smile flickered briefly over his face before he straightened and pulled her to her feet. Clasping her hand, he strode down the driveway at a pace that convinced her he was determined not to give her a chance to change her mind.

He continued to grip her hand when they stopped outside the front door, and he reached forward to press the doorbell. It was answered almost immediately, and the door swung open to reveal a tall, good looking man with dark hair and the same green eyes as Luke, his face breaking into a grin when he realised who it was.

"Luke." He grasped Luke's outstretched hand and pulled him into a bear hug before stepping back and scrutinising him closely. "You look like hell!"

He turned his gaze to Chloe and smiled, holding

out his hand in a rather gentler manner. "And you must be Chloe."

She gave an uncertain smile and looked across to Luke as he spoke quietly. "This is my brother, Callum."

"Are you going to invite them in or spend the entire day on the doorstep?" A female voice floated in through a doorway off the hall.

"Sorry, we're coming now," Luke called back as he acknowledged his brother's rueful smile.

Chloe allowed herself to be ushered through to the bright, airy living room, still trying to process what this might mean. There, sitting on a large, comfy chair and bottle feeding a baby, was the woman she immediately recognised from the wedding video. Sara looked up and smiled as they walked in.

"Oh, I'm so pleased you came."

"Chloe, this is Sara, my sister-in-law," said Luke, the ghost of a smile lifting the corner of his lips when he saw comprehension dawn in her eyes.

Sister-in-law? Oh God, how could she have been so stupid?

She tried to cover her surprise and confusion as Sara carefully handed the baby over to Callum—"here, you can take over"—before enveloping her in a baby powder-scented embrace. "I've been dying to meet you. Luke has told me so much about you."

Sara turned to kiss Luke on the cheek before hugging him tightly, a slight frown marring her brow as she cupped his cheek with her hand. She was clearly shocked by his weary appearance.

"Why don't you go through to the garden, and I'll bring us something to drink?" She ushered them out through the patio doors, and Luke led Chloe down the terraced garden to a shaded patio area at the bottom. They sat on a beautifully ornate wrought iron bench, but he made no attempt to touch her, simply resting his arm along the back of the seat.

"Why didn't you tell me?" She whispered. "Why did you let me think…" Her voice tailed off.

"That she was my wife?" His voice was curiously flat. "You didn't give me a chance. You wouldn't listen, wouldn't let me explain."

"But…on the beach, you should have just told me." She bit her lip, thinking back to that night, how desperate she had been to stop him from speaking, from lying to her. "You could have shouted over me, anything. But you didn't. You didn't say anything."

He gave a humourless laugh. "Shouted over you? Really? You think that is acceptable? Chloe, you made it perfectly clear that you wouldn't believe anything I said. Everything was a lie, remember?"

He was right and she knew it. Her cheeks burned with shame. "But…this morning at Mum's, and in the car driving up here…you could have told me, said something."

"Would you have believed me?" His gaze was fixed on a point at the bottom of the garden. "I guess I could have tried. But, you know, I was just desperately hoping that at some point you would tell me it didn't matter where I was taking you, that you trusted me, that you knew I wouldn't do that to you.

"But you didn't. You went on believing the worst right up to the point I introduced you to my sister-in-law."

He turned to look at her then, and her heart sank when she saw the emptiness in his gaze. "At no point did you think of any reasonable explanation for what you saw. Chris could have been lying about when it was taken; it could have been a few years ago and I could be divorced or, God forbid, a widower. Or it could have been my sister-in-law. A really simple, obvious explanation that any reasonable person would think of. You knew I had a brother; knew I'd been to see him recently. But it didn't occur to you, did it? It didn't occur to you that I could be anything other than a lying bastard. You didn't give me a chance."

She lifted a trembling hand to her mouth. *How could she have been so blind, so cruel?* Luke had never given her cause to doubt him and yet, at the first test, she had failed him. She looked up to meet his gaze, and her stomach twisted at his guarded expression.

"I'm so sorry. You're right, about everything, of course you are. And there's nothing I can say to take it back. I wasn't thinking straight, I know that's no excuse." She said quietly. "But I was so happy, and then Chris forced his way in, said you were using me, said…the usual things. And then he showed me the DVD and…I don't know…it seemed to confirm what he said. It's so much easier to believe the bad things."

Luke gave a weary sigh, rubbing his hand across his face and leaning his head back to catch the sun. "I know."

"I should have trusted you," she acknowledged quietly.

At first, she thought he wasn't going to respond, but eventually he straightened up to look at her and shook his head slightly. "The thing is, I'm not sure you can bring yourself to trust anyone."

She felt a stab of fear at the finality of his words,

and tears filled her eyes. He was slipping away from her, she could feel it. She opened her mouth to deny his words, but before she could speak, he got to his feet and she blinked in surprise. *Was he leaving?*

Scrambling from the seat, she was about to run after him when she saw Sara walking down the garden towards them, carrying a tray laden with biscuits and a huge jug of fresh juice tinkling with ice cubes. Luke took the tray from her and set it down on the garden table. Callum was following close behind, carefully carrying the baby and winding him against his shoulder as he did so.

"Well, you've certainly brought the weather with you." Sara smiled, and took the seat opposite, reaching up to take her son from Callum.

"So how is the little one?" asked Luke, leaning over to allow the baby to grasp his finger. "He's changed even in the fortnight since I saw him."

"He's doing fine," said Sara, smiling proudly down at her baby son. "I could do with him sleeping a little more at night, but I have to admit Callum does his fair share."

"What's his name?" ventured Chloe, struck by the tenderness in Luke's face as he bent over the baby.

"Daniel, after his grandfather."

"Oh, that's lovely." She smiled.

Sara returned her smile and then wrinkled her nose. "And with exquisite timing, Daniel has decided two minutes' rest is all I needed. If you'll excuse me, I'll go and change his nappy."

Callum immediately got to his feet. "You stay there, love, I've got this." He took the baby from his mother, and turned to grin across at Luke. "And uncle here can help, it's about time he got a little more hands-on with his nephew."

"A little peace at last." Sara heaved a sigh of relief as they left, and settled back into her chair, fixing Chloe with a curious but friendly stare. "So, you're Luke's mermaid?"

"I…I'm what?" She blinked.

"When Luke first moved into the cottage, he told us about this beautiful, red-haired girl he saw on the beach every morning. He was captivated apparently but, by the time he got down there, you'd always disappeared, and he decided you must be a mermaid," said Sara. "Did he never tell you?"

Chloe shook her head in surprise, not sure how to respond.

"You know you're the first girl he's ever allowed us to meet?" Sara said quietly, after a pause. "He's never been serious about anyone before."

"I'm not sure he is serious about me," she said with difficulty, tracing the delicate ironwork of her seat with the tip of her finger. "Not in the way you mean. He's always made it clear he doesn't want a long-term relationship, that he's not looking for commitment. I know his business takes up most of his time."

Sara gave a sigh and leaned forwards in her seat, glancing up the garden to make sure Luke was still in the house. "Has he told you about his parents?"

Chloe nodded. "Yes, I know the whole thing affected him badly. I understand his mum had a breakdown, and he was caught up in the middle of it. He's told me on a few occasions that he doesn't ever want to be responsible for hurting someone like that; it's why he's been very honest with me about not wanting to get into a serious relationship."

Sara shook her head impatiently. "But it's more than that. Yes, he's terrified of hurting someone, of course he is. And, you know, there's nothing wrong in what he does, which is to make sure he doesn't lead anyone on. But Callum and I have talked about this a lot. We think he was affected far more than he realises. It's not a case of working hard and playing hard, of not having the time to put into a relationship. He's frightened of opening himself up to someone, because if he does that, he runs the risk of being hurt himself, of going through what his mum went through."

Chloe stared at her thoughtfully, remembering the vulnerability she had seen just before he kissed her, and the guarded expression in his eyes a few minutes earlier when he told her he thought she didn't have the ability to trust anyone. It had never occurred to her before that he might be as frightened of failing someone as she was.

"Look, I've only just met you, Chloe," said Sara softly, reaching across to touch her hand briefly. "And I don't want to pry, but…you love him, don't you? I can see it in your eyes."

She frowned, dropping her gaze to her hands. Was she really so transparent? "Yes."

"And he is crazy in love with you, too. So, don't push him away."

As Sara relaxed back into her chair, Chloe stared at her in surprise. *Was that what she had been doing?*

She looked up when the two men returned from the house, Callum carrying a small baby monitor.

"Daniel's gone off to sleep," he said, placing the monitor on the glass table in front of him. "You girls okay?"

"We're absolutely fine, thank you, darling," smiled Sara. "Much better now you boys are here, of course."

Luke took his seat next to Chloe, once again resting his arm across the back of the seat, but she felt the gulf of space between them as if it were a gaping chasm instead of just a few inches. She ached to reach out to him, to try and break down the barrier that seemed to have been erected, but she didn't know how.

Conversation flowed easily around her, but she took little part in it and could only sit there, desperately unhappy and wondering how things could have gone so wrong in such a short space of time.

"Hey."

Luke's fingers brushed her shoulders and she looked up in surprise to find they were alone. Callum and Sara had obviously gone into the house. "You okay?"

She nodded her head, closing her eyes when he hooked a finger under her chin.

"Look at me," he said softly.

She reluctantly met his gaze, but his face blurred and shimmered as tears filled her eyes. She felt him pull her close, holding her tightly as she sobbed into his neck.

"It's okay," he muttered softly, stroking her hair. "Look, Sara and Callum are fixing an early tea, but if you want to go, I'll take you back to your mum's."

Suddenly terrified that he would drop her off at her mother's house and she would never see him again, she slipped her arms around his neck. "Not yet, please don't take me back yet."

He reached up to unclasp her hands, gently

brushing her tears away as he leaned back to look at her.

"I'm so sorry, Luke. I didn't mean what I said. I didn't mean it. About you hurting me, knocking some sense into me," she gabbled desperately, cupping his face with her hands, searching his eyes for understanding. "You'd never hurt me, or anyone, like that, I know that. I know it. I never thought for a moment you would. I was just so angry, I didn't know what I was saying. I'm so sorry. Please, say you'll forgive me."

He held her gaze for the longest time, but she could read nothing in his eyes, and then he covered her hands with his own, turning his head to kiss the palm of her hand.

"There's nothing to forgive," he said at last. "Look, let's forget about the last few days and this morning. It's a lovely, sunny afternoon, and Sara and Callum are very good company, so why don't we just enjoy the next couple of hours?"

Again, that shiver of fear as his words hinted that she was losing him, despite Sara's thoughts to the contrary. But she was tired of weeping pathetically in his arms, knew he must be weary of it, too. So, she straightened her shoulders, wiped her eyes, and gave him a bright smile.

"Okay, I'm sorry."

"Okay." He drew her to him, placing a lingering kiss on her lips before taking her hand and walking back into the house. "And stop saying you're sorry."

****

It was early evening when they finally climbed

back into the car, and Chloe turned to wave as they pulled away from the kerb. When they were out of sight of the house, she settled back into her seat and turned to Luke.

"They're both so lovely, thank you for taking me to meet them." She winced, suddenly remembering the reason why Luke had brought her to meet his brother and sister-in-law.

He caught the change in her expression and reached across to squeeze her hand. "They liked you, too."

He remained quiet and withdrawn on the journey home, and she was reluctant to break the silence. Again, she sensed his withdrawal from her, and the closer they got to her mother's house, the more nervous she became. When they eventually pulled up outside, he switched off the engine, but made no move to get out.

She licked her lips, her mouth suddenly dry. "Luke, I know I've messed things up—"

"Wait." He cut her off, closing his eyes for a second before taking a deep breath. "I think we should take some time out, not see each other for a while."

He held up a hand when she started to respond. "I've arranged to do some work back at the Warwick Company head office for a few weeks. Hardaker's is in a fairly good place at the moment, so it's about time I concentrated on some of the other businesses."

The pain ripping through her took her breath away, her voice away, and she could only stare at him in silence, agonizing shudders wracking her body. She simply sat there, unable even to see his face clearly through the tears that streamed from her eyes.

"I'll be away from the cottage for a while," he

continued, with obvious difficulty.

"Don't do this. Please don't do this," she whispered.

He reached for her hand, squeezing her fingers painfully. "I have to."

"No, you don't. No, you said you wouldn't hurt me. You promised me." She swallowed painfully. "You promised me."

"Chloe, you have no idea…" He broke off when his voice cracked. "I don't want to hurt you, but it doesn't seem to matter what I do, I hurt you anyway. And I don't want to. I don't want to, because…I love you."

She drew in a ragged breath of surprise, hope flaring at his words. Hope that quickly faded when he shook his head sadly and, taking her hands in his, leaned forward to rest his forehead against hers. "But I can't spend the rest of my life trying to prove it to you, trying to prove that you can trust me."

"You won't have to." She shook her head. "I know I messed up, but I love you and I do trust you."

"Listen to me. I love you, and I want to spend the rest of my life with you," he said clearly, lifting her face to his so he could look into her eyes. "But I need to know that it's what you want, too. You have to decide if I'm really what you want, if you can trust me, if you want to be with me. I'm giving you time to think about that."

"But I don't need time. I know that already," she cried, pressing his hands closer to her face. "I love you. I want to be with you."

He carefully withdrew his hands from hers. "I need to know that you've really thought about what that means. I can't go through another weekend like this last one, Chloe. I know you have good reasons for not trusting anyone, but I couldn't love you any more than I do now. And you need some time to decide if I'm what you want."

She stared at him through her tears, unable to believe he was telling her to leave.

"Luke…" She couldn't manage any more.

He leaned across to kiss her, a lingering, heart-breaking kiss that ended far too soon when he reached across to open her door, before retreating to his own seat and staring through the windscreen. There was an air of finality about his actions, and she had no choice but to step out onto the pavement. The engine fired into life immediately, and the momentum of the car shooting forward slammed the door shut as she watched him drive out of her life.

Chapter Thirteen

"Chloe?"

How long she had been standing on the pavement, Chloe had no idea. But on hearing her name, she looked up and saw her mother in the doorway to her house.

With some effort, she forced herself to walk up the drive, reaching out for her mum, and sobbing into her neck as Claire folded her arms around her daughter.

"Don't worry, darling," she whispered against her hair. "It's all over. You're better off without him. He was hateful."

Chloe recoiled immediately, staring at Claire as if she were a stranger. "You really can't help yourself, can you?"

Angrily dashing away her tears, she pushed past her mother and ran up the stairs to the spare room. When she returned ten minutes later with her overnight case, Claire was standing in the living room, arms folded across her chest.

"That was incredibly rude." She moved her shoulders and sniffed disdainfully. "I was being supportive."

"Supportive?" Chloe managed a humourless laugh. "You've never been supportive, Mum. You've just kept on drilling into me how awful men are, and how rubbish I am at being a woman."

"I never—"

"And that man..." She pointed through the window, her finger shaking with suppressed anger. "That man is good, and kind, and respectful...and he loves me. He doesn't think I'm rubbish...at all."

"Then you haven't learnt anything." Claire dismissed with a sneer. "You didn't hear the way he spoke to me, the things he said."

"I can guess what he said to you. And I would imagine every word of it was true. You're a bitter, selfish woman, who can't bear to think of me being in a happy and loving relationship. You want me to grow old, as lonely, and bitter as you. Well, I won't. I refuse to end up like you. Do you hear me? I won't!"

With that, she turned her back on Claire, picked up her overnight case, and strode to the front door. "Come on, Jasper. We're leaving."

****

It had been a long week, and Luke was glad to see the back of it. Throwing himself into work had eased the pain of their last weekend together, of the memory of Chloe's stricken face when he had left her at the side of the road. It was difficult to believe it had only been a month ago. In one way, it seemed to be an age, while at the same time, it was as if it were only yesterday.

There was a chill in the air, despite the sun, and he recognised with some surprise the muted colours of autumn when he looked out across the cliff tops to the sea. The seasons had changed in the month he had been away. Arriving back at his cottage late last night, he had not yet ventured down to the beach. He hadn't since that awful night they had argued, and this morning he'd chosen instead to walk along the winding path that eventually led to the village.

Making his way back to the cottage, he was aware of the tension pulling across his shoulders and unsettling his stomach, and he chewed his lip. What if he had been wrong? What if he had made the biggest mistake of his life, and now Chloe had second thoughts about wanting to be with him?

He had done a lot of thinking himself over the last few weeks, acknowledging what a change she had wrought over him. He remembered clearly the first time he had viewed Fulmar Cottage, with the intention of renting for a short period while he worked with the management team at Hardaker's Shipbuilding Ltd. to try and steer the company back into profit.

The estate agent had shown him around the cottage, which had been up for sale or let, allowing him to wander around the garden. He had noticed the sandy path at the edge of the small front garden, and followed it to where it reached the cliff edge and dipped down, continuing its winding path down to the beach.

That was the first time he had seen her, standing close to the shore, unmoving and gazing out into the ocean. The wind had caught her hair, lifting it out behind her in a fiery mass, and moulding her long skirt to her legs, the material pooling into a short train at her feet. She had looked for all the world like a mermaid from tales of old, and he had been unable to tear his gaze from the mesmerising image. The insistent voice of the estate agent had eventually broken the spell, and he had turned to him blankly, asking him to repeat his question. By the time Luke had been able to look back at the beach again, the girl who had enchanted him had vanished.

Back in the kitchen, when the estate agent began his spiel about needing to know fairly quickly if he wished to go ahead with the lease, Luke had surprised both himself and the young man by saying he wanted to buy the cottage, immediately offering to pay the full asking price. It was difficult to say who had been the most taken aback by his spur of the moment offer, but the estate agent recovered quickly and made the phone call there and then, determined not to lose his commission. Luke's next move was to offer to buy out Hardaker's, yearning suddenly for stability, for something substantial, something that he could work on for himself rather than working to drive though changes for someone else's company.

Shaking off those memories, he looked up as the roof of his cottage came into view, and he paused uncertainly, listening hard. He could have sworn he heard a dog barking. He looked around, expecting to see someone out for a walk, but he was alone. He could see for miles, and there was no-one else around. Shrugging it off as unimportant, he returned to his thoughts and continued along the path towards his cottage.

Crunching up the gravelled drive, he stopped in his tracks when Jasper came racing around the corner, tail wagging ten to the dozen. His heart missed a beat, before beginning to thump frantically in his chest. Chloe must be waiting for him in the garden. He resisted the urge to turn and retrace his steps. What if his risk had backfired? What if she were here to tell him she had made a mistake? That she didn't want to be with him?

Breathing long and slow, trying to ignore the

churning sensation in his stomach, he straightened and walked slowly around the cottage to the garden at the back.

****

Chloe drew her feet up on the bench—the same one she had used that day after the storm—and hugged her knees to her chest. She had been sitting there for over an hour, and had grown cold in the chill morning air. She closed her eyes and rested her head on her knees, drifting in and out of daydreams. It had been the longest month of her life, and one of the most difficult, although perhaps some good had come out of it. Whatever Luke had said to her mother had clearly struck a chord. The weekend after Luke left, Claire had turned up unexpectedly at Chloe's cottage.

It had been long, long week, and Chloe was simply going through the motions: get up, go to work, come home, go to bed…repeat. She was numb, hollow, and unable to believe that Luke was no longer a part of her life. Desperate for some message, some sign that he wasn't gone forever, she had texted Scott and asked him to let her know when Luke returned to Hardaker's.

A knock on her door that Saturday afternoon saw her leaping from the sofa and running to the door. No-one ever called to see her unexpectedly; it had to be Luke. She threw open the front door, her emotions spilling over with relief and happiness, but instead of Luke, it was Claire standing on her doorstep.

"Mum?"

To her amazement, Claire's chin began to tremble, and her blue eyes filled with tears. Not once in all her years could Chloe ever remember seeing her mother cry.

231

"You'd better come in."

By the time they were settled in the living room, Claire had composed herself once more, but she appeared softer, more vulnerable than before.

"What is it you want, Mum?"

"To say I'm sorry." She lifted her chin and met Chloe's gaze. "You were right...partly. Perhaps I may have been a little bitter and selfish, but I never, never meant to make you feel...worthless."

She spoke quietly and vehemently, leaning forward and reaching out her hand. "All I ever wanted was to try and stop you from going through what I went through. It never occurred to me that I was...that I made you think you were somehow less of a woman."

Chloe stared at her mother's hand, but made no move to take it. "What was I supposed to think? You told me so often that we don't have what men need, we're not the type that good men want. It was never about you, it was always us."

"Oh, Chloe—"

"Do you know what that did to me? How it made me feel?" Her fingers shook with nervous energy; she had never spoken to her mother like this, but she was determined not to back down now.

Claire looked away in discomfort. "I'm sorry."

"I believed you, believed I was worthless. But I wanted to prove you wrong. When I met Chris, he was so lovely at first. But before long, he began to tell me how rubbish I was, how stupid. Everything you made me feel, he made me feel, too. You were right."

"Stop it!" Claire stood up, her hands over her ears, tears spilling down her cheeks. "I don't want to hear it."

"And then I met Luke. And it was so different,

Mum. He made me feel special, normal, like a woman. He made me believe I wasn't worthless." Chloe smiled through her own tears. "He loved me."

Mother and daughter had talked long into the night—sometimes arguing, sometimes crying—until, mentally and physically exhausted, Chloe had shown Claire into the guest bedroom before falling into her own bed.

The heart-to-heart discussions had begun again the next morning until, at last, Claire had turned to her daughter. "If he loved you, why did he leave you?" The defiance, the bitterness was gone. Just a genuine question.

"Because I'd hurt him, with my lack of trust, with my inability to believe that any man could truly want me. I pushed him away."

"But can't you tell him? Can't you get him back?"

"I hope so. I'm going to try." She lifted a trembling hand to rub her forehead. "He's gone away for a while, given me time to work out what I want."

"But you already know what you want." Claire offered her an understanding smile. "You want him, don't you?"

When Chloe nodded, Claire looked down at her hands. "I'm so sorry. I didn't realise how much I was hurting you, damaging you even. I thought I was protecting you."

"I know, Mum." At last, she reached across to grasp her mum's hand. "But you have to stop. You can't tell me that you want to be like this, to be so angry and bitter and resentful towards every man. To be alone. You can't."

"He made me like this." Her soft voice quivered

with anger.

"But he's just one man." Chloe insisted. "Don't you remember what it feels like to be in love? To be so excited, and nervous, and scared when you know you're going to see the person who makes your tummy turn over? You must have felt like that before…Johnny." She could never bring herself to call him her father.

Claire was silent, and concentrated on stroking the top of Chloe's hand with her finger. Eventually, she looked up with a shy smile. "I remember. It doesn't feel so long ago, when Sandy and I were getting ready to go to the nightclub, when we thought we might see him. And then, oh the feeling when we got there, and there he was. He made me feel like I was the most beautiful girl in the world."

"Don't you want to feel like that again?" Chloe squeezed her mother's hand. "You're still young, Mum; still so pretty. You deserve to meet someone, to be happy. What Johnny did was awful, but it was so long ago and there are so many lovely men out there."

"But what if he was right? You don't know the things he said that night."

"I can guess. In fact, Chris has probably said them to me, too." She could understand her mum's fear, still battled with it herself. "But, Mum, when it's with the right person, it's so different. It's wonderful. Don't be that bitter, resentful person. Don't let him win."

"I don't know how to be any different. It's who I am now."

"Rubbish," Chloe said softly. "You can be whoever you want to be."

"Do you really think so?"

"I do." She moved closer to her mother on the sofa.

"I know it won't be easy, but I'll be here. And I think it's something we both need to do."

It had taken a while to convince her, but Claire had eventually agreed to seek counselling. Worried that her mother's determination would wane, Chloe had attended the initial meeting with her, and they were now waiting for an appointment for the sessions to begin in earnest. Under no illusions that it was going to be anything other than a long and painful journey, nevertheless Chloe felt optimistic that she had begun building a more positive relationship with her mother. Claire was still struggling to come to terms with her past, but appeared determined to move forward at last.

For her part, Chloe was no longer fearful of what Chris may or may not do. She had seen the recognition in his eyes on that night in her cottage, seen him realise she no longer feared him, and knew he had lost his control over her. She didn't know what had happened between him and Luke, and she didn't need to know. Chris would never bother her again; he was a coward, and she was far stronger than he would ever be. This time it was real.

Over the last year, she had told herself over and over again that he had no power over her, but she had never truly believed it. Not until now. Now, she was free, and it felt wonderful.

A prickling sensation along the nape of her neck brought her back to the present, and she forced her eyes open, blinking slowly as the image of Luke swam into view. She stared for a moment, thinking it was another daydream, until Jasper barked expectantly and broke the spell. She scrambled to her feet, the sudden movement causing her to stagger when a wave of dizziness swept over her, and Luke grasped her arm to steady her.

She wanted to step into his arms, but his expression was shuttered and unsmiling, and she felt a thrill of fear. She was too late.

"You're cold," he said softly. "You'd better come in."

****

Chloe watched him move around the kitchen, busying himself making drinks. Only when he passed her a steaming mug of coffee did he sit down opposite, and finally meet her gaze.

"How did you know I was back?"

She could feel the warmth staining her cheeks. "I asked Scott to let me know. He sent me a text this morning saying you'd called in at the office yesterday afternoon."

When he remained silent, she tried an apologetic smile. "I'm sorry, I should have called you rather than just turning up. I just wanted to see you."

A brief smile flickered over his features, but his expression remained wary. "Have you been okay?"

She nodded, cupping her hands around the mug, and shivering as the warmth began to seep into her fingers. "I've been sorting things out with mum. For the first time in my life, we sat down, and we talked. Talked about...everything; the things she had gone through, how that had made her feel."

She looked up at him. "I don't know what you said to her, but it certainly gave her pause for thought. How she made me feel." The last was said in a whisper,

Luke remained silent, his gaze never wavering from hers as she continued. "Anyway, I think she's finally acknowledged that I'm not her, and that I need to live my own life however and with whoever I want. We've even arranged to get some counselling." She looked up at him with a slight smile. "I thought about what you said. I've looked at myself and my life; at what it is I really want. And I know what I want."

This was it. Everything they had gone through up until now had been leading to this moment. She blinked when he pushed himself away from the table to lean against the worktop, his arms folded across his chest as he waited for her to speak.

Painfully aware of Sara's warning, of the potential fear hiding behind his guarded expression, she moved to stand in front of him.

"Luke, my feelings for you haven't changed. I'm lost without you. You make me whole." She tentatively touched his face with her fingertips. "Please let me in, let me love you. Don't let me be too late."

He reached for her, pulling her to him and lifting her off her feet as he buried his face in her neck. She could feel the shudders running through him.

"I thought I'd lost you," he whispered against her shoulder. "I've missed you so much. Chloe, my fate was sealed from the very first moment I saw you on that beach."

He set her gently back on her feet and cupped her face with his hands. "I fell in love with you in an instant. I just couldn't bring myself to believe it."

Weak with relief and happiness, almost unable to believe what was happening, she slipped her arms around his waist, resting her head against his chest. "I love you, Luke. I love you, I love you, I love you."

He laughed softly, tightening his arms around her.

"Is this the same girl who sat in my kitchen and calmly told me she didn't believe in love?"

She pulled away to look up into his amused gaze. "And is this the guy who equally calmly told me he wasn't looking for a long-term relationship? That he wasn't ready to fall in love?"

He grinned, linking his arms loosely around her waist. "*Touché*. I guess we were both kidding ourselves."

Chloe nodded and stepped closer, sliding her hands across his chest, and reaching up until her lips were just millimetres from his. "Just so we're clear then. Are we saying this is serious? A long-term thing?"

"I've never been more serious about anything in my life," he answered softly, closing his eyes when her hands continued to move across his chest, up over his shoulders, and across his back. "And if you're going to continue to talk to me, you'd better stop what you're doing with your hands, because I can't concentrate."

She giggled, brushing her lips against his. "Just because we're serious though, it doesn't mean we can't have some fun, does it?" She stepped backwards out of his embrace.

"Absolutely not."

He reached for her as she danced out of his grasp, running for the door and out onto the path. "But you'll have to catch me first!"

Chloe ran down the cliff path, gasping as Jasper galloped past her. She had a good few seconds' head start, and Luke only managed to catch up with her as she reached the beach. He caught his foot on the uneven ground, stumbling as his arms closed around her waist, and they fell back onto the sand in a tangle of arms and legs.

Rolling onto his side, he brushed the hair from her face, and the love she saw shining from his eyes brought tears to her own. In that moment, they both knew it was going to be all right. She had found a man she could trust, and Luke had finally found his mermaid.

A word about the author…

I love to write heartwarming, contemporary romance and romantic suspense novels, with characters I really want my readers to engage with. I live in the beautiful East Riding of Yorkshire in the UK and, although I work full-time in the public sector, my favourite pastime, when not writing, is wandering around old stately homes and fantasizing about a fairytale life.

I enjoy engaging with both readers and other authors, and am a proud member of the Romantic Novelist Association.

http://elliegrayauthor.wordpress.com